TCR

PAUL DUFFÉ

Karen Laurence Sneed

Paul Duffé

Special thanks to Elizabeth Copley for her generous editing services, Ryan Schinneller for the cover art and continuous technical assistance, Kevin L. Sneed for the internal illustrations, and especially Tor.

Chapter

1

"There he is!"

"Where?"

"Over there. Behind that box. Get him!"

In a flash the skinny black and white cat shot out from behind the box and right through the younger Animal Control officer's legs. Before he could turn around, the cat was down the alley and across the street.

"You fool! You let him get away," barked his portly boss. "Which way'd he go?" He was red faced and irritated.

Both officers were on a mission to round up stray cats and dogs in the neighborhood of Springfield in Jacksonville, Florida. The once thriving neighborhood now consisted mostly of rundown homes occupied by low income residents as well as a growing population of stray and abandoned animals. In an attempt to help with Springfield's cleanup and restoration, the city's government ordered Animal Control to assist residents. Several packs of dogs had been reported as well as numerous feral cats. Having been assigned to the Springfield animal removal operation, Ben Daniels and Lyle Fields were doing their best to locate and capture as many animals as possible. Having seen a black and white cat walking down an alley, the two parked their truck and attempted to corner it.

"It took off across the street," said Ben, the young officer.

"I see him. He went through the fence in front of that big house. Come on, I think we can get in over by the driveway," replied Lyle, the boss.

The large house was built in the Victorian style of the early 20th century and was surrounded by a thick brick wall and rod iron fencing. At one time it was the grandest house in city. Hidden behind decades of overgrown vegetation weaving between the elaborate ironwork, the home stood proudly representing an age that had long since passed.

As the two officers reached the driveway, they were stopped by a large, black man holding a shovel. Usually the gates were closed, but this morning, Thomas Jones, was attending to grounds keeping duties along the driveway and had them open.

"Can I help you?" Thomas asked, blocking their access to the property.

"Out of our way, boy. We're rounding up stray cats and dogs. A cat we're chasing just ran through the gate and onto this property," Lyle said. His condescending tone was not lost on Thomas. Thomas did not move.

"I'm sorry, but this is Miss Emma's house and she don't like strangers on her property."

"Is that so?" Lyle asked. Thomas was a big man, but that didn't stop Lyle from inching his way up to him. Spittle shot from his mouth as he talked.

"How would you like to go to jail for obstructing official business of the Department of Animal Control?"

"No sir. I don't want to go to no jail, but Miss Emma is very particular about who's allowed on her property. She won't like seeing strangers roaming all around."

"Don't worry, boy. You leave her to me." Lyle pushed past Thomas with Ben following close behind.

"Who's this Miss Emma anyway and why would anyone with this kind of dough want to live here?" Lyle asked when out of earshot.

# # #

The 1971 Pontiac Catalina looked noticeably out of place as it cruised through the streets of the dilapidated Springfield neighborhood. Looking out the car window, 86 year old Emma Perkins sighed as she watched the scenery pass by. It always brought back memories from long ago.

Emma's father, Cecil J. Carson, was a respected businessman in Chicago, Illinois. Having built a successful hardware business, Cecil and his young wife Eleanor were well known throughout their community. Chicago was a thriving city in the early 1900's and the Carson's were among its many beneficiaries. Though Eleanor was a formidable woman and devoted mother and wife, her health was fragile. Chicago winters were not for the weak and from her early childhood, Eleanor was plagued with respiratory problems. Cecil did all he could to make the harsh Chicago winters as tolerable as possible for her, but she fought ever-worsening illnesses during the winter months.

One winter five years into their marriage and after the birth of their third child, Eleanor came down with pneumonia. Cecil was beside himself with worry and spared no expense in getting her whatever medical care she needed. She had had pneumonia before, but, this time it was bad. The doctors did all they could. When she fell unconscious, they told Cecil nothing more could be done. She was in God's hands now.

Cecil prayed day and night for a miracle. Finally, Eleanor began to slowly recover. Relieved, Cecil swore that he would never let this happen again. Acting on the doctor's recommendation, he decided to move his family to a warmer climate.

Cecil was familiar with the small city of Jacksonville, Florida because two years earlier newspapers were filled with articles about a devastating fire which consumed almost two thirds of the city. Aid was requested and sent from all over the country for the stricken residents. Cecil shipped materials to Jacksonville almost since the first requests were made. He also made it a point to travel to Jacksonville after the fire to get a firsthand account of what was needed. While there, he made important contacts and helped set up a critical building materials distribution network. He became widely respected and his help valued. After returning to Chicago, he continued to invest in the devastated city and help from afar. Then after almost losing his wife to the harsh Chicago winter, his mind was made up. It was time to relocate and Jacksonville was their destination.

By early spring and well into Eleanor's recovery, Cecil set out to find a house for his family and begin setting up his new business enterprise in Jacksonville. Having already built a successful hardware company in Chicago, he expanded and opened his first branch in Jacksonville. Three years after the fire, rebuilding was underway throughout the city, but the recovery was slow. Cecil was able to acquire a large lot where he built the new store and warehouse. Before it was officially opened, he was besieged with orders. Because of his connections, he was able to bring a wide variety of building materials to the city and within weeks his business was thriving. By late summer the family arrived. Cecil rented a home in the beautiful Riverside area, but after the family settled in, it became obvious that the house would not accommodate their growing family for very long. By fall, he and Eleanor discussed building a new house.

The Springfield neighborhood was considered highly desirable by the locals. Cecil managed to buy an entire block peppered with huge live oaks. He wanted to build the most extravagant home the area had ever seen. To accomplish this, he brought his friend Marshall McKinley down from Chicago. Marshall was well-known throughout Chicago for having designed some of the most beautiful and stately mansions in the city. He wasted no time designing a grand eight bedroom, seven bath Victorian home surrounded by lavish gardens. He was able to save and incorporate the existing beautiful century-old live oaks into his design so flawlessly that they and the home seemed as if both had always co-existed. Cecil told Marshall that money was no object and he wanted a house that would stand the test of time. Using many new building techniques available, the house was well-constructed of steel, brick, concrete, quality wood and even had electricity, gas, and indoor plumbing. Jacksonville was familiar with all these modern conveniences but lacked the infrastructure to make them widely available to the general population before the fire. However, after the fire, an entire new sewer system and electrical grid were constructed in order to make access to these conveniences readily available to everyone.

By spring of the following year the home was completed. Surrounded by an ornate brick and rod iron fence encompassing the entire block, the home was the grand jewel of Springfield. Though other residents also built impressive homes throughout the neighborhood, the Carson House, as it came to be known, was the most impressive. Its four massive turret-like round rooms made it look more like a castle than a house. People walking the sidewalks would often be seen standing on the other side of the ornate fence marveling at its beauty.

As Cecil's business continued to grow, so did his family. By the late 1920's, Cecil and Eleanor had produced nine children. Emma, was the youngest and the last. Growing up in such opulence and splendor shielded her from the harsh world that existed outside the home's gilded fortress like gates. Here, in the heart of Springfield, Emma enjoyed the innocence of childhood and watched as her father's role in the city's growth and prosperity thrived.

In 1925, Cecil ran for mayor and won. Many residents said the city was fortunate he was at the helm during the Great Depression that followed the stock market crash of 1929. Due to his business experience and background, he was able to keep Jacksonville from suffering the devastating financial setbacks so much of the rest of the state and country experienced. Because of his outstanding leadership, he was repeatedly elected mayor until his death in 1939. By then, Emma was a young woman and had traveled the world with her parents.

Emma was never one for the conventional. She was a strong-willed, prideful woman. Probably because she was the youngest, her father doted on her the most. She idolized her father and learned much from him. Roles for women were limited at that time, but her father constantly encouraged her to buck the system and be her own person. It often caused many an argument between Cecil and Eleanor, but Cecil stood his ground. He knew Emma was an exceptional young woman and wanted her to have all the opportunities available to her.

Unfortunately, after Cecil died in 1939, tension between Emma and her mother only grew worse. Having been raised in a more traditional way, Eleanor wanted her to find a husband and start a family. But, it was not what Emma wanted. Having already had a taste of the world when traveling with her parents, she craved more. The tension continued between her and her mother until 1940 when she left to become a nurse in the US Navy. For Emma, this was the perfect escape. She could travel and continue seeing the world while also serving her country.

Emma had just completed her first year of nursing school when Pearl Harbor was attacked. She was thrust into the action ready or not. Needing all the trained nursing personnel available, Emma was sent to the Pacific Theater and served in all capacities for the duration of World War II. Rising quickly through the ranks, by the war's end she had reached the highest level of command possible for a woman in the armed services at that time. Emma served proudly in the Navy until she retired in the early 1970's. After a brief marriage, she was offered the opportunity to run a prominent nursing school in Maryland where she worked for another 20 years before finally retiring to her family home in Jacksonville.

With a mix of disgust and sadness Emma turned away from the depressing scenery to face the woman driving her car.

"What a pity. This use to be such a beautiful area of town. Now look at it. Riff-raff all over. Rundown homes, closed up businesses, my father is probably spinning in his grave! I need to call that lazy no good mayor again and give him a piece of my mind," she said. She crossed her arms and bit her lower lip like she always did when she was angry.

"You know good and well he won't take your calls anymore. After your last conversation with him, I'm surprised he didn't get a restraining order against you," her driver said.

"Me! Against me?" Emma sat straight up and adjusted her blouse. "That pin-headed little twit doesn't have the guts."

Lightly chuckling, Cathy Barton shook her head in agreement. "No, he probably doesn't."

Cathy Barton was not only Emma's permanent live-in care giver, but also her closest friend and confidant. Twenty years Emma's Jr., Cathy and Emma met while serving in the Navy.

Cathy was a foster child raised in a broken system moving from family to family until she turned 18. For an unmarried woman her age at that time, opportunities were limited. It was not in her nature to work in manufacturing, nor did she desire office or clerical work. Having few choices, she decided to join the Navy and become a nurse.

Times were different then and nursing was one of a few professions where women were valued and treated with the respect they deserved. Because her education was limited, she had to work harder than most to get by. Fortunately, her first boss was Emma. Emma respected the young woman and was astonished by her drive and commitment. As much of a struggle as it was, Cathy never gave up and always pushed herself. This level of commitment got Emma's attention and soon she took the young woman under her wing.

Emma had joined the Navy many years prior to Cathy. Haven risen through the ranks, she was a senior officer and commanded a large number of nurses and other medical personnel. Knowing Cathy's troubled background, Emma took a liking to her and over time became a mentor and guiding hand. They developed a strong bond. Cathy became the daughter Emma always wanted and Emma was the mother Cathy never had. As the years passed, they made it a point to try and be assigned together whenever possible. After Emma retired, Cathy continued in the nursing profession. But when Emma's health began to deteriorate, she decided to retire so she could help Emma with her ever growing medical needs.

One critical need was transportation. After being forced to give up her driver's license years earlier, Emma relied on Cathy to get her to her appointments and take her shopping. For a time, the neighborhood lived in constant terror of Emma and her large car, never knowing when the Pontiac might suddenly emerge on a particular neighborhood street. Emma claimed she had no need to be driven. But for the neighbors, this was a different story. After many fender benders and other minor collisions, it wasn't unusual to hear neighborhood residents shouting warnings to each other when her car would be spotted moving through the streets. "Look out! Here comes Miss Emma!!" would be heard preceding her arrival by blocks.

As the Pontiac turned the last corner before reaching her driveway, Emma noticed the parked animal control truck across the street.

"Huh!" She gestured toward the truck. "They should be catching the riff raff around here and leave the poor animals alone."

The large car entered the open gates and was met by Thomas who had a strange look on his face.

"What's wrong with him?" Cathy asked, slowing and putting down Emma's window to address their long time yardman and ward.

Thomas lived in the caretaker's cottage on the property. He was considered "simple minded" by many in the neighborhood, but Emma believed him to be autistic. As a favor to his father, Emma allowed Thomas to work and live on the property with him and after his father passed away, Emma took it upon herself to see to Thomas's care. She allowed him to live in the cottage and even paid him in return for taking care of the property. Thomas was devoted to Emma and Cathy and looked after the landscaping and house with meticulous attention to every tree, flower, and blade of grass.

"What's wrong with you this morning? You didn't mow over another one of my flowerbeds again did you?" Emma asked him.

Looking down, Thomas twiddled his large thumbs nervously.

"No Miss Emma. All your flowers are okay," he said and went silent.

"Then what is it?" she asked. Her tone suggested she had not gotten over her irritation with the dilapidated neighborhood. Thomas sensed it and his lip trembled.

"I don't want to go to jail Miss Emma! The man said I could go to jail if I didn't let them in to catch a cat. I don't want to go to jail!" He looked at Emma with wide, frightened eyes.

"Jail? Who said you were going to jail?" she demanded. Before Thomas could answer, they saw the black and white cat running from around the side of the house and dart under the stairs leading to the front porch and main entry. Ben came running after the cat with a net. Taking up the rear was the large, heavy, badly out of shape Lyle cursing and barking orders to his younger subordinate.

Emma's eyes narrowed as she ordered Cathy to continue up the driveway to the main entry. Before the car came to a stop, she was already out and demanding to know what was going on. For an 86 year old woman, she made a formidable site. Ben froze in place, but Lyle continued approaching.

"No need to worry ma'am. We're with Animal Control. We're here to collect that stray cat there under your porch." Completely dismissing her he turned to Ben.

"Well? What are you waiting on? Don't just stand there looking stupid. Get him," he said pointing to the stairs.

"You will do no such thing," Emma said, slamming the metal cane she was leaning on into the pavement to get their attention. "I did not give you permission to enter my property and I want you to leave."

Ben started to walk away when Lyle ordered him to freeze.

"We'll be leaving just as soon as we capture that cat, ma'am," said Lyle.

Cathy was now out of the car leaning on the open driver's door. When hearing Lyle dismiss Emma's order she grinned and looked down at the pavement shaking her head. "Wrong answer," she whispered under her breath. Thomas had walked up the driveway and was standing next to Cathy.

"You and your associate will be leaving now and I'm not going to repeat myself," Emma said.

"Ma'am, you're interfering with a direct order from the mayor and city council. Step aside and let us do our job."

That was the last straw. Emma's eyes narrowed and her posture became erect. She didn't look like the fragile 86 year old woman she was. Instead, she had transformed into the sternest school-teacher-military-drill-sergeant one had ever seen.

"Listen to me you disgusting, slob of a little man. I don't give a good goddamn what that pinhead prick of spoiled brat mayor ordered. And I care even less about that corrupt excuse for a city council. You forced your way on to my property threatening my groundsman with jail so you could illegally trespass to capture that animal. You are not the police and have no warrant or legal reason to be here so you can leave now on your own or you'll be carried out feet first." With that, she pulled a small caliber hand gun from her purse. "Now get off my property," she said pointing it at them.

"Screw this! I'm not getting shot over some cat! I'm out of here," said Ben taking off down the driveway.

Putting his hands in the air, Lyle's voice trembled. "Ok! You win. We're going. You're crazy lady," he said walking by her with his hands still in the air. In one last act of defiance he shouted back, "Keep the damn cat! I hope it gives you rabies!"

Emma pointed the gun at him like she was going to shoot. The frightened officer took off through the open gate much faster than anyone thought he was capable of moving.

She put her gun back in her purse and made her way to the stairs where the cat could be seen looking out from between the steps.

"Well, come out so we can get a better look at you," she said addressing the cat. Lightly meowing, it hesitated for a second then squeezed out from between the steps and approached Emma. Using her cane to support herself, she leaned down to pet the animal. "My word. You're a skinny thing. Bet you haven't eaten in a long time. Come on in and let's see what we have for you." She carefully made her way up the stairs and entered the house with the cat following, tail straight in the air.

"If she plans on keeping that cat, it's getting a bath first," Cathy said reaching into the car to get the rest of their items.

"Do you think Miss Emma would've shot those men?" Thomas asked wide-eyed.

Smiling, Cathy threw the carry bag over her shoulder. "These days, I don't think so, but twenty years ago? Absolutely."

Chapter
2

Cathy wasn't kidding about giving the cat a bath. After he was feed and she and Emma had dinner, Cathy picked him up to examine him. They were surprised by how docile he was. Purring as Emma scratched him behind his ears, Cathy gave him a good looking over in an attempt to examine him for injuries, fleas, or other parasites he might be infected with. After satisfying themselves that the cat was amazingly clean, Cathy opted to give him a bath anyway, just in case. Clearly not happy with the experience and despite a very unhappy expression on his face, he showed amazing patience while being bathed. As Cathy was drying him off, Thomas knocked on the kitchen door and Emma let him in.

Thomas updated them that the plantings along the driveway were complete and that he was finished with his work for the day. He saw Cathy drying the cat.

"Is you really gonna keep that old cat?" Thomas asked.

"Well, as much as anyone can keep a cat," Emma said watching Cathy work him over with a dry towel. "Cats are fiercely independent, Thomas. I've always believed they pick who they want to live with and for whatever reason this guy has picked us. So sure, he can stay as long as he likes."

"What are you going to name him? If you're gonna keep him, he has to have a name."

"You're right," said Emma. Looking at Cathy, "Any ideas?"

"Nothing comes to mind. How about you Thomas? What do you think?"

Thomas scrunched his face as he thought. "He looks like a skeleton with those black and white markings. Let's call him 'Skelator'. That's the name of an action figure from the He Man cartoons," he said proud of his suggestion.

Cathy and Emma smiled to each other. Thomas was a full grown man in his early-forties, but he had the mind of a child. He still enjoyed watching cartoons and playing with the same action figures his late father bought him when he was very young.

"I'll never remember that name," Emma said as she prepared a plate of food for Thomas. "How about we just call him Tor for short?" She gestured for Thomas to come sit at the table and eat his dinner.

"I like that. Short and sweet. Easy to remember," Cathy said. She put Tor on the floor letting him go.

Tor walked over to Thomas and rubbed against his legs purring loudly. Thomas looked down at him and rubbed him behind his ears. "I like that too. That's a good name for you cat. Tor."

"Tomorrow we'll get him a collar and a tag with his name and address on it in case those two jackasses come back and try to catch him again," Emma said getting up from the kitchen table. She was tired and ready to turn in. It had been a long day and she was ready to call it a night.

"I'll clean up the kitchen and put the cat out, then be up to help you to bed," Cathy said.

Emma looked down at the cat. "Welcome to our family, Tor. Nice of you to join us." She said good night to Thomas and started down the hall to the elevator.

"She looks tired tonight," said Thomas. Cathy heard the concern in his voice.

"She had a long morning of tests and doctor appointments. I think the day finally caught up with her," she said hiding her own concerns from Thomas. She knew he thought of Emma like a mother and cared deeply about her.

After he finished his dinner, Cathy said good night to Thomas and put Tor out. Standing on the back porch, Thomas looked down at Tor. "You

can stay with me if you want Mr. Tor. Come on. I'll show you where I live."
He led him back to his small gardener's cottage.

Chapter
3

The cottage was a small, one bedroom one bath bungalow nestled into a secluded corner of the property. Hidden behind a jungle of greenery, it was built shortly after the main house was completed and originally used by the house staff. As live-in staff became less common, it was later turned into a permanent residence for the groundskeeper. Because the house and property required an enormous amount of upkeep, this proved to be a good decision.

After Emma's mother died in the early 1960's, the house was left to Emma in a trust. All of Emma's older brothers and sisters had either passed away or moved and started families elsewhere. As the last unmarried sibling, Emma was granted the right to live in the home until the time of her death at which point the house was to be deeded to the city along with a substantial trust intended for its upkeep if Emma chose to do so.

Once Emma began her career in the Navy, her visits home were less frequent. Emma enjoyed traveling the world and learning about different people and their cultures. Settling down and starting a family was never a priority which was often a source of heated debate between her and her mother. Eleanor was a "traditional" woman and constantly nagged Emma about getting married and giving her grandchildren. She looked down on women who were independent and career-minded believing them to be of a lower class and neglecting their duties as a woman. To Eleanor, a woman in the workforce in any capacity was a disgrace in her opinion and having a daughter as a nurse was an embarrassment. Emma's father, however, recognized a fire in her and throughout her life constantly made it a point to encourage her to not let anything stand in her way. But sadly, after he passed away, the relationship between Emma and Eleanor only grew more strained.

Emma would stay away for long periods of time to avoid the unpleasant encounters the two would have when she did visit.

While stationed in Germany in 1962, Emma received news that her mother had passed away. This came as a shock since her mother said nothing about being sick in letters or occasional phone calls. If anything, since moving to Florida so many years earlier, her mother had hardly been sick a day in her life. The sudden news saddened Emma as well as caused her to feel some amount of regret for not having had the chance to try and mend their relationship. And having not seen her mother in over two years, the sting of her passing was all that much harder to take. Arranging for the first transport back to the United States, Emma was stateside and back in Jacksonville in less than a day.

When she arrived at the house she was surprised to find the main gates open and the property wildly over grown and un-kept. She also noticed a gathering of cars in the driveway, but didn't pay it much attention and figured people had stopped by to pay their respects. When she entered the house she was greeted warmly by her mother's housekeeper and caregiver, Wilhelmina Jones. Wilhelmina was a young black woman in her late 20's and had been working for Eleanor for the past five years. Her help and services had proven to be invaluable. She not only saw to the house work, but also cared for Eleanor and cooked her meals. It was Wilhelmina who found Eleanor and called Emma.

Emma looked around the house and realized she and Wilhelmina were the only ones there. "Who do all those cars belong to?" she asked.

Wilhelmina hesitated, staring at the floor. "Those cars are friends of Mr. Davis," she finally answered.

"The groundskeeper?" Emma asked. "Is he still here? The property looks terrible. Why does it look so bad?"

Fidgeting, Wilhelmina was uncomfortable answering Emma's question. "Ever since he said he hurt his back he hasn't been doing much of anything with the grounds. Mostly he just stays in his house. We only see him when he comes to collect his check."

"And why are his guests in the main driveway?"

Again hesitant to respond, Wilhelmina could not look her in the eye. "This is Saturday. They always come to play cards with Mr. Davis on Saturday."

"Cards? Did you say cards? My mother died less than a day ago and he's holding a card game in the cottage?" Before the sound of her voice went silent, she was out the door and heading down the gravel path to the groundskeeper's cottage with Wilhelmina doing her best to keep up.

As she got closer to the cottage she could hear music and voices. It all sounded very festive. Infuriated, she banged on the door with her fist before opening it and walking in. Someone removed the needle from a record player so fast it scratched across the record. Silence.

Emma's presence was formidable. Standing five feet seven inches tall and dressed in her naval officer's uniform, she commanded attention just entering the room. Mr. Davis stood and started babbling incoherently. He was somewhat intoxicated, but sober enough to know he had a problem.

"Enough! I don't want to hear your bullshit," Emma said as she held up her hand shutting him up. "For your information Mr. Davis, as of my mother's passing, this house is now mine and my first act as the new owner is to fire you! Now get your personal belongings and get the hell off my property! All of you!" She held the door open as one by one Mr. Davis's guests ran out of the house. Wilhelmina stood off to one side of the path. Her eyes were huge. She had never heard a woman talk to any man like that.

"Now come on, honey. Surely we can work something out," Mr. David said as he approached Emma.

Emma's eyes narrowed. "On second thought, leave your personal belongings and get the hell out." With that, she grabbed him by his dirty shirt collar and tossed him right out the front door. He hit the ground hard before managing to stand. One of his guests ran back to him and forced him down the path and away from her. This was probably fortunate for Mr. Davis, since Emma held a black belt in karate and was well-trained in a wide variety of other hand-to-hand combat techniques.

Wilhelmina stood speechless.

Emma walked back inside to assess the state of the cottage. It was a mess. "Look at this place! The man's a slob. I can't hire a new grounds keeper until this place is cleaned up."

An idea popped into Wilhelmina's head. "Oh, oh, Miss Emma, I have an idea. My husband Thomas is a good man and is good with plants and he can fix anything. He'd be perfect for the job!" Wilhelmina was so excited she was bouncing and smiling like an excited little girl. The sight amused Emma and calmed the fire burning within her from her encounter with Mr. Davis.

"Do you think he would want the job?"

"Oh yes, Miss Emma. He's very handy with tools and use to keep up the golf course at that fancy country club on the Southside."

Emma saw this as a solution to multiple problems. "Great! He's got the job if he wants it. And you both can live in the cottage here on the property, too. I'd feel better with the two of you around to look after the place when I'm not here."

Wilhelmina was so excited she couldn't contain herself and hugged Emma tightly bouncing up and down. Emma was amused and hugged her back.

"Now, the first thing we need to do is drag a hose in here and hose down this whole place. And I'm still not sure that'll be enough to wash away all signs of the former Mr. Davis."

# # #

While Emma over saw the arrangements for her mother's funeral, Wilhelmina was hard at work cleaning the cottage. As a favor to Wilhelmina and Emma, Thomas went to work restoring the grounds around the property. Emma and her mother may not have been close, but she respected how beloved her mother was by the community and knew of all the hard work she and her father had done in helping raise the city from the ashes many decades ago. Thanks to Thomas, the house and grounds again stood proud as Emma invited many members of the community to take part in a final tribute to her mother.

After the commotion around her mother's funeral died down, Emma had Thomas and Wilhelmina over for dinner. She wanted to thank them for all their help and told them as long as she lived and owned the house they were welcome to stay and live in the cottage. They worked out a fair salary arrangement.

It also turned out that Wilhelmina and Emma had something in common. Wilhelmina was a midwife - one of the best in the city. This was not a skill one learned in school, especially for a young black woman. It was a time honored position passed down through the generations from her mother to her. Even though Wilhelmina had no formal training in the medical field, what she did know astounded Emma. Emma respected her skills and knowledge even if others in the community looked down on women like her.

Over the years, Wilhelmina was midwife to hundreds of women, both black and white. Even professionals in the medical community would occasionally call on her to help when they had patients in trouble. Wilhelmina's experience proved invaluable and many of them owed her for helping teach them and further their careers.

Unfortunately, the one person Wilhelmina could not help was herself. Even though she and Thomas had tried to get pregnant for years, it never seemed to be in the cards. Then, unexpectedly, in her late thirties Wilhelmina became pregnant. They both believed it was a miracle from God. But the pregnancy was not easy. Emma was the director at the nursing school in Maryland when she got the news that Wilhelmina was having difficulty with her pregnancy so she took an extended leave and returned to

Jacksonville to see it through with her. It was fortunate she returned when she did because one week after arriving and a month before her due date, Wilhelmina went into labor. Her blood pressure was dangerously high so Emma used all her clout and was able to get Wilhelmina admitted into a local Navy hospital where the doctors performed an emergency C-section in order to save both their lives. Wilhelmina gave birth to a slightly premature baby boy that they immediately named Thomas Jr.

It wasn't long before they noticed that something was different about Thomas Jr. Though he appeared healthy physically, something seemed "off" about the baby boy. By age 2, it was obvious young Thomas was showing signs of slower mental development. Still, Wilhelmina and Thomas Senior doted on him constantly. Emma, too. By his third year, it was clear Thomas Jr. had a mental disability. Doctors believed he would never progress beyond a fifth or sixth grade education.

Near Thomas' fourth birthday, Wilhelmina fell ill. She was diagnosed with advanced ovarian cancer. Within three months, she passed away. Thomas Sr. was devastated. Emma had returned home and helped see Wilhelmina through her final days and vowed to help Thomas look after Thomas Jr. To Emma, Thomas Jr. was like a son.

Emma assured Thomas Sr. that they would always have a home on the property and even had the conditions of the trust adjusted so that they would be taken care of in the event something happened to her. When Thomas Sr. passed away, Thomas Jr. was a young man in his early twenties. He might not have had a formal education, but he had proven to be a great student. His father taught him all about carpentry and landscaping. Thomas was well prepared to take over the care and upkeep of Emma's house and property if he so desired.

Shortly after Thomas Sr. passed away, Emma decided to retire. She was now in her seventies and had been running the nursing school for almost twenty years. Knowing Thomas Jr. was alone, she returned to Jacksonville for good. She was also concerned about the neighborhood. Springfield had been in a state of decline for decades. She worried something might happen to Thomas Jr. and thought it would be better if she was there permanently. She made it clear to Thomas Jr. that the cottage was his and that he was responsible for its up keep. He understood and took meticulous care of it. He was proud of his work, landscaping, carpentry, and always enjoyed showing others the fruits of his efforts. And Tor was no exception. As Thomas led Tor down the path to the cottage he talked to him as if he was another person.

"Come on Mr. Tor. I want to show you where I live. But, you have to promise not to make a mess. Mrs. Emma says no messes are allowed." Tor trotted behind Thomas with his tail up. The two walked together like good friends who had known each other for many years.

# # #

The cottage was small and cozy. It had a simple lay out of two bedrooms and one bathroom with an open-space multi-use room including a tidy kitchen, living area and dining space. For Thomas, the space was more than enough. He made it a point daily to see to its upkeep. Emma had offered numerous times to buy him new furniture, but Thomas politely declined. What memories he did have of his mother and practically all of his father revolved around life in this sweet little cottage. He still referred to several of the items as his mother's or father's. Taking such good care of the cottage and its contents was his way of preserving the memories he had of his parents. Emma understood, but still made it a point to ask.

After cleaning up, Thomas took his favorite book from a large and tightly over-packed bookshelf in the living room. Even though he barely read at a six grade level, he loved to try to read and look at the pictures. Settling into his favorite spot on the couch, he opened the book and flipped through its pages. This was his favorite book because it was about animals from all over the world. His father bought it for him many years ago and would often sit and read to him about the animals while Thomas looked at the pictures. He turned to the section about cats.

"Look, Mr. Tor. This is what you are. You're a cat." He turned the book toward Tor to show him a picture of a domestic house cat. Tor was lying on the couch next to Thomas bathing himself. He looked up at Thomas and meowed lightly. Thomas smiled back – he was happy Tor was there. Thomas continued looking through the book and sharing pictures with Tor until he eventually dozed off with the book on his lap.

Around 11pm Thomas was awakened by something pawing his leg. He sat up slowly, stretching and yawning. Tor ran to the front door and started scratching it and meowing loudly.

"Oh, Mr. Tor! I'm sorry! I forgot you need to go out." He quickly got up and opened the door.

"Good night, Mr. Tor," Thomas said standing in the doorway watching Tor stroll away on the path. "See you tomorrow. I have to go to bed now. It's way past my bedtime," he added before shutting the door and turning in for the night.

Chapter
4

Tor walked down the gravel path into the darkness and sat down. Looking around, he let his eyes adjust as he sniffed the evening air and listened to the sounds of the night. Springfield was located just outside the urban core of downtown Jacksonville. The large overgrown brick and iron walls surrounding the property did a remarkable job of keeping out the noise of the busy world beyond them. Here, an oasis of serenity and nature existed. For Tor, this was a new world to be explored. Hearing a sound off in the distance he ventured out to discover its source.

# # #

Emma couldn't sleep as she tossed and turned in her bed. She had been experiencing more sleepless nights over the past several months. After recently turning 86, she found herself contemplating life and death with a greater frequency. Emma had no real regrets about how she lived her life. Like most, she recalled decisions that if she could do them over she certainly would have made different choices, but for the most part, she looked back on her long life with a sense of pride and accomplishment. Still, she grew more concerned as she realized the end was growing closer. Sitting up in her bed she felt warm and decided to open a window. She knew Cathy would be cross with her for getting up without help, but she didn't care. Reaching for her cane, she used it for support as she carefully made her way over to a sitting area in her bedroom by one of the tall Victorian windows. The sitting area was unique in that it was a rounded section of the room. From outside, the house looked like a castle. Four large three-story turret like structures formed the corners of the house. Emma's room was part of one of these rounded structures and she used it as a sitting area. Two chairs with a table between them faced out so she could sit and look into the gardens. As she slid the window up, it made a screeching noise that made Emma cringe, because she thought it might wake Cathy. After satisfying herself that she was safe, she stood at the window feeling the cool night air on her face.

Looking out into the dark gardens she saw the shape of the gazebo in the distance and smiled. Remembering back to a crisp autumn day in the 1960's, Emma remembered how happy she was. It was true, at least in her case, the happiest day in a woman's life was her wedding day.

She closed her eyes and relived the brief ceremony presided over by a Navy Chaplin and how they had to rush him through so they could make a flight to Paris.

Emma met her future husband, Allen Perkins, while she was in the Navy. Allen was a famous doctor known the world over for his pioneering research in genetics. They had a long distance relationship marked intermittently by periods of living together, but soon their careers would again pull them in different directions. It was an on-again-off-again relationship that continued for almost 20 years until Emma retired from the Navy. After Emma retired, she returned to Jacksonville to settle down and relax before writing the next chapter of her life.

Passing through Jacksonville on his way to a conference in Orlando, Allen decided to surprise Emma. He turned a three-day visit into a month long escape. While there, he and Emma decided it was time to write the next chapter of their lives together. It seemed fast, but, the reality was they had known each other for years; the time was finally right. Allen had a speaking engagement in Paris that he could not miss so they decided Paris would be the perfect honeymoon.

During their first year, they were inseparable. They lived out of hotel rooms traveling the world together for Allen's work. Emma proved invaluable in helping with his research and engagements. They were a powerful couple and lived life to the fullest. But, just at the beginning of their life together, tragedy struck.

After a speaking engagement in London, Allen was being driven back to his hotel when his car was struck by another vehicle. He was killed instantly. Emma was devastated. Again, she found herself pulled back to her family home in Jacksonville where she grieved in a semi-state of seclusion for weeks.

Giving up and hiding from life was not who Emma was. Knowing of her recent tragedy, a friend and colleague suggested she be considered for running a prestigious nursing school in Maryland. When the Board made her the offer, Emma jumped at the chance. She needed to get back into the world and doing something she loved was the perfect opportunity.

Standing at the window looking at the gazebo, she realized she was smiling. Allen was truly the love of her life and she felt fortunate to have nothing but happy memories of their time together. She was about to turn away from the window when she noticed something moving on the ground in the garden. Focusing, she recognized Tor. He heard the window screech and was investigating. He looked up and saw her standing at the window looking down at him. She waved a friendly hello.

Tor meowed lightly and looked around studying the area. He went to a large oak tree and climbed straight up it to a limb drooping over the porch roof that extended from under Emma's window. When he got close enough, he effortlessly jumped to the roof and trotted over to Emma.

"Wow! I'm impressed. You did all that to come see me?" Emma asked. She gently stroked Tor down his back; he responded to her loving touch and rubbed against her. "Well, you might as well come in and take a load off young fellow." Emma left the window open so he could leave if he wanted and made her way carefully back to bed. When she climbed in, she propped herself up slightly and pulled the covers up. Not really tired, she reached for her book and picked up reading where she had left off hours before.

Feeling a thud, she looked over the top of her book to find Tor standing on the end of her bed. She lowered the book and patted the covers next to her. "Come on up, boy." Tor walked over and let her scratch him on his neck. He curled up and settled down next to her. Emma could hear him purring. "Poor fellow. Out there all alone. Well, rest assured, you have a home now."

Tor's purr was soothing to Emma and it wasn't long before she drifted off into a deep, restful sleep.

Chapter
5

Emma woke the next morning feeling refreshed. She couldn't recall the last time she slept so soundly. Remembering Tor, she looked around the room, but did not see him. Noticing the open window, she hopped out of bed and started walking over to close it. She paused for a moment when she realized she was not using her cane. "I'll be damned," she said turning around and looking at her bedside table where the cane was still leaning. Feeling stable, she shrugged and continued to the window with confidence. Looking out, she saw Thomas tending to his weeding duties around the gazebo and Tor lying on a lawn chair watching him. Looks like Thomas has a new friend, she thought. This pleased her to no end.

Deciding not to wait for Cathy, she began her morning routine. Emma was an early riser, but Cathy was not. Often Emma would wait in her bed reading or watching TV until Cathy came to check on her. It took a little doing, but soon Emma had fixed her hair and dressed herself. Feeling empowered, she made her way downstairs to the kitchen and started preparing breakfast.

Smelling coffee brewing, Cathy followed the aroma to the kitchen. She stopped dead in her tracks by the sight before her. Emma had prepared a large breakfast - bacon, sausage, scrambled eggs, toast - the works. The kitchen table was set and juice had been poured.

"Oh, there you are," Emma said turning around and noticing Cathy looking at her with an astonished expression. "Be a dear and call Thomas and Tor to breakfast will you? She dumped another pile of bacon on a plate and turned back to face the stunned Cathy. "Is everything okay?"

Cathy shook off her stupor. "My, my, someone's in a good mood today." She did as instructed and called the two to breakfast.

Thomas came in first followed by Tor. Stunned surprise showed on his face as he stood frozen taking in the scene before him. Tor ran over to Emma. Purring loudly, he excitedly rubbed against her and occasionally stood up on his back legs.

"Easy, boy," Emma said looking down and laughing at his excitement. She reached for a smaller plate. "Here you go. I made a plate especially for you." She put the plate on the floor; Tor immediately devoured the sausage and bacon she had given him.

Cathy and Thomas were still dumbstruck. They hadn't seen Emma this active in years. "What are you two looking at? Don't just stand there gawking, sit down and eat something." Before either one of them moved Emma hastily added, "Thomas, wash your hands first."

The four of them enjoyed breakfast together. Tor lay next to Emma sharing her bench seat. The mood was upbeat and good-spirited with Emma leading much of the conversation. Thomas and Cathy kept exchanging puzzled looks, but neither was about to say or do anything to dampen the celebratory atmosphere. While cleaning up, Emma informed Cathy that she wanted to go with her when she went to get a collar and tag for Tor. She also wanted to do a little shopping while they were out.

Cathy's expression, again, gave away her surprise. Usually Emma could barely muster up enough strength to go to her doctor's appointments. To want to go shopping was completely unexpected.

"And we need to pick up some cat food, too. I don't plan on cooking for Tor every morning."

# # #

Emma had Cathy on the go for most of the morning. After getting a collar and a tag for Tor at a local pet store, Emma insisted they go shopping for clothes at one of her favorite stores in Riverside. Having been awhile since she'd spent any time in Riverside, Emma was amazed by how much it changed. New stores and restaurants had sprung up all over. The aroma of all types of foods – ethnic and conventional - filled the air. By noon, Cathy was dragging and Emma noticed. Using the excuse that she needed to rest, they sat down for lunch at a small table in the shade of a large oak tree outside a quaint café. Both ordered a small meal and something refreshing to drink. The weather was perfect for a spring day and it was nice to be out of the house. For nearly a decade Emma had been mostly housebound. Being out, enjoying the day and people watching was a wonderful change of pace.

Riverside was an older area of the city like Springfield. However, unlike Springfield, the renovation and restoration movement had been going strong for much longer. Dotted with several parks, small businesses, and homes, the area was transformed into a trendy and desirable location to live and shop. It was especially popular with young professionals; the neighborhoods of Riverside were alive with activity. Seeing the large number of people walking and cycling delighted Emma.

"Isn't this wonderful Cathy? Look at all these people. And all these businesses! I just can't get over how much things have changed over here." It wasn't that long ago when most of the buildings were boarded up and the homes were falling apart. Emma looked like an excited child as she took in the sites.

"It is wonderful, but expensive. Real estate has gone through the roof. You're right, it's a great area. You have parks, entertainment, and food, all within walking distance from your home. You don't get that with the new developments outside the city. And the historical groups have done a good job of keeping new development to a minimum or at least making it look like the older buildings and homes in the surrounding neighborhoods. But unfortunately, it seems now the demand is greater than the supply. People are finding it harder to buy homes here because of the limited supply and ever increasing real estate prices."

"Wouldn't it be great if our little corner of Springfield could undergo such a transformation? I mean look at our area. We have parks and some beautiful old homes that could use preservation and restoration," Emma said. She had a gleam in her eye Cathy had not seen in years. Cathy knew that look well. In her younger days, when Emma had an idea, she was known to move mountains to achieve her goals.

Since Emma had been mostly housebound for the past several years, she'd missed much of what was going on in her own neighborhood. Cathy filled her in on the on-going efforts to rehab Springfield. A preservation group as well as a citizen's organization were created to give more exposure to their efforts. Unfortunately, both organizations were small and not as well organized as what they had in Riverside.

"On the way home we'll drive back through some of the renovated neighborhoods so I can show you what's been going on. I think you'll be surprised. Still, unlike over here, there's a lot of work that needs to be done," Cathy said.

Emma twisted her sunglasses around in her hand as she looked out across the busy sidewalk occupied with people enjoying the delightful spring day. The corners of her mouth pulled back.

"I know that look. What's going on in that head of yours?" asked Cathy. She sat forward in her seat preparing herself for whatever Emma had on her mind.

"It's been some time since we've hosted a social event in the old Carson house. I think it's time we reintroduce ourselves to the neighborhood. Sounds like the preservation society and the citizens group could use a little help. Let's invite our counsel representative, heck, invite the ones at large too as well as that little twerp of a mayor and the members of the citizens group and the preservation society. I want to get a better feel for who's doing what and find out who the major players are leading restoration efforts on our side of town. Maybe we can do something to spur things along a bit." Emma spoke with confidence reminiscent of her military days.

Unable to contain herself any longer, Cathy finally broke. All morning Emma had been running her ragged. And now, suggesting they host a party, this was the last straw.

"Okay, level with me. Who are you and what did you do with the old lady? What's gotten into you today? Did you mix up your medication? And if you did, can I try whatever it is you're on?"

Emma laughed. It had been a long time since she'd been able to surprise Cathy with anything. "I don't know. I just woke up feeling refreshed. It's strange I know. But I'll tell you one thing, I'm not going to waste this energy sitting on my can at the house." Standing up she continued. "Let's go. I want to see those areas of Springfield you were talking about. But, first we need to go to the grocery store. I want to pick up something to cook for dinner." In her younger days Emma enjoyed cooking for people.

Still sitting, Cathy looked up at Emma completely in awe.

"Come on, Cathy, pick up the pace. What would people say if they knew you were having trouble keeping up with an 86 year old woman?" Emma asked as she started walking toward the car.

# # #

Tor had been following Thomas around the yard all day as Thomas did his landscaping duties. Since the house and property occupied an entire block, daily work was necessary. When Thomas got to a particular bed of flowers that grew from bulbs, he was disappointed to find that many had been up-rooted during the night. Holding his head, his frustration was obvious. "Oh, no! A mole!" Thomas looked at Tor and explained to him as if he was a person capable of understanding what he was saying. "Moles are bad for these flowers, Mr. Tor. They dig up the plants while looking for bugs. Now I have to replant all these bulbs! I hate that mole! He's always messing up my flowers!"

Tor walked over smelling the ground around the damaged areas as Thomas got a small garden spade from his wheel barrel/garden cart. He used the cart to transport his tools and equipment around the property. Suddenly, Tor's ears perked up and he cocked his head to the right. He heard something on the edge of the bed. He crouched down and slowly made his way toward the area of interest. In one pounce Tor jumped over a border of low Aztec grass and leapt hard on to a soft area of dirt. He dug frantically kicking dirt out in all directions. Thomas watched confused. "What are you doing Mr. Tor? Don't be digging holes all over the place. I'll have to fill them in."

But Tor was undaunted by his request. A few seconds later, he plunged his head in the hole and went motionless. Thomas scrunched his face as he wondered what he was doing. After a few seconds of complete stillness, Tor pulled his head from the hole with a dead mole in his mouth.

"Mr. Tor! You got that bad old mole! Good for you!" Tor walked over to Thomas and lay the dead mole down on the ground. "Good boy. Mr. Mole won't be messing up this flower bed again." Tor was energized and swatted at the dead mole. Noticing his playful energy, Thomas kicked it into the yard and Tor took off chasing it. He did this a few more times to indulge Tor before returning to his replanting duties. Eventually Tor tired of his mole and took up a position in the shade bathing himself not far from Thomas.

For the rest of the afternoon Tor kept Thomas company, occasionally chasing grasshoppers and lizards until Thomas called it a day and went back to his cottage to clean up before dinner. Hearing Cathy and Emma arrive home, Tor joined them in the driveway and followed them inside.

# # #

Dinner was served on the same cozy kitchen table they ate breakfast. The much larger formal dining room was rarely used. As with breakfast, Emma prepared most of the meal herself. Having been some time since she'd put a dinner together, she chose to keep it simple and made spaghetti with her special homemade sauce. Cathy prepared salads and baked fresh bread. Cathy also enjoyed baking. It had been sometime since she'd indulged herself. Tor not only had his own cat food, but Emma kept giving him small helpings of meat and sausage which he happily ate.

Over dinner, Emma presented Tor with his new collar. It was a thin black break-away collar that was designed to come off if it got hung on something. They also had a small brass tag made with his name and the address of the house on it. After placing it on Tor, Emma stood back and said, "Very handsome." The collar went well with his mostly black coat and he didn't seem to mind wearing it.

Tor looked like a statue as he sat on the bench seat next to Emma. Cathy remarked at how regal he looked. "He looks like an Egyptian statue the way he's sitting, almost like he's protecting you," she said.

Emma reached over and gently stroked his head and back. Immediately, he started purring and rubbed against Emma's hand acknowledging her affection. "Welcome to our little family, Tor. We're all friends here," she said as she gently smiled at him. He looked up at her; she would have sworn he was smiling back.

Emma always tried to make it a point to involve Thomas in their conversations believing the more social interaction the better. But this night she didn't need to do much prodding. Spaghetti was his favorite and Emma's was the best as far as he was concerned. Thomas's excitement was obvious.

Emma and Cathy chatted about the party they wanted to put together informing Thomas that they were planning to have guests in the coming weeks and wanted to spruce up the property and house a little. Not that it needed much work since Thomas did a good job of keeping things looking nice. Still, Emma wanted to add a few more touches here and there. Thomas was excited and looked forward to the work.

"And Mr. Tor can help me like he did today."

"He did? When I saw you two this morning he looked like he was lying around watching you. How did he help?" Emma asked.

Thomas could barely contain his excitement. "He killed a mole. The same mole that's been messing up the flower beds. Mr. Tor dug him right out of the ground and got him! He also got some of those big grasshoppers. He stayed with me all day! I hope he'll help me out some more tomorrow."

Cathy and Emma exchanged surprised looks. "Do moles carry rabies?" Cathy asked.

Emma rolled her eyes and stood up to start clearing the table. "One less mole is a good thing. Sounds like Tor is trying to earn his keep. Keep it up, boy," Emma said, patting him on her way to the sink.

Thomas and Cathy insisted on clearing the table and told Emma that that was enough out of her for the day. Surprisingly compliant, Emma agreed and called it a night. When they were alone Thomas and Cathy discussed how good she looked. Neither could remember the last time they had seen her in such high spirits. After cleaning up, Cathy said good night to Thomas. She looked down at Tor as they were walking out. "Emma's really taken a liking to you, Mister. Thanks for coming into our lives." Almost as if he understood her, Tor rubbed against her legs before following Thomas out the kitchen door.

Tor hung out with Thomas in his cottage throughout the evening. From his vantage point on a large comfortable chair he watched Thomas play with his toys and action figures on the floor. Even though Cathy and Emma had bought him new toys over the years, these were his favorite since they were gifts from his father. Time passed quickly when Thomas played. He had a lively imagination and used it effectively creating all kinds of fun scenarios. Hearing the clock chime, Thomas knew it was bed time. He cleaned up his toys and started toward his bedroom. Remembering that Tor needed to be put out, he walked him to the front door. Standing in the doorway, Thomas waved excitedly at Tor as he passed by into the darkness. "See you tomorrow Mr. Tor. Thanks for your help today." He shut the door and turned off the light.

Tor sat on the small patio outside the cottage listening to the sounds of the night. It wasn't long before he noticed movement by a pile of overturned flowerpots. He froze and crouched down. It was a mouse. Tor went motionless. His black coat and white markings blended him seamlessly into the shadows. The mouse disappeared behind the underbrush next to the patio. In a flash, Tor pounced. A faint squeak could be heard followed by a dim glow that briefly illuminated the dark corner before it faded. Tor emerged carrying a small mouse. Proud of his kill, he left it on the door mat for Thomas to find in the morning.

# # #

After turning in, Emma lay in her bed thinking. From the time she woke up she felt good; better than she had felt in a long time. Wondering what changed she decided not to question it. At her age, time was a blessing. Emma was not afraid of death. She had long since made her peace. Her greater concerns were for Cathy and Thomas. They were her family and she wanted to be there for them as long as she could. Feeling a little warm again, she decided to open the window. When she reached the window she was surprised to find Tor standing there.

"This is a nice surprise. Come in. You know you're always welcome."

Tor jumped from the window ledge to the floor. After exploring the room, he hopped up on the bed. Like the night before, he settled into a position next to Emma and curled up lightly purring. Smiling, she reached over and patted him affectionately. As if a switch flipped, his purring became louder. The sound was soothing so she lowered her book and shut her eyes. Listening to the gentle rhythm, she soon drifted off into a deep restful sleep

Chapter
6

Emma wasted no time getting down to business. From her many years in the Navy, she knew if she wanted to revitalize her little corner of Springfield she needed a plan. That morning she took a chance and invited Jon Sanders, one of the more influential members of the Jacksonville Historical Society to her home for lunch. He accepted immediately. When Cathy announced that Jon had arrived, Emma met him on the front porch.

"Emma Perkins. It's always nice to see you. I have to say, I was surprised to get your invitation to lunch," he said embracing her with an affectionate hug. Pulling back he looked at her. "I don't know how you do it. You just keep getting younger every time I see you."

"Enough with the flattery. You're making an old woman blush," Emma said. Taking him by the arm, she led him into the house.

Lunch was served in the more formal dining room. It was simple yet elegant. Emma knew Jon loved her home for its historical and architectural significance and she enjoyed sharing it with him. She rarely used the room, but for him she made an exception. Not one to banter around the subject, Emma wasted no time getting to the point.

"So Jon, Cathy and I were having lunch the other day in Riverside and I was amazed to see how much it's rebounded. The area was so alive. Restaurants, shops and people were everywhere. It reminded me of how Springfield use to be when I was a child. On our way home, Cathy drove me around some of the Springfield neighborhoods that have been renovated. I can't tell you how delightful it is to see so many of the older areas coming back." She explained how it gave her the idea to encourage the same kind of restoration or renovation in Springfield.

Jon had known Emma for many years. He also knew Emma had been slowing down mostly because of age and health issues and rarely made public appearances. Hearing that she had recently lunched in Riverside surprised him and when she announced that she wanted to be more involved in restoration efforts in her area, he was momentarily dumb struck.

She saw the expression on his face "Don't look so surprised. This old lady still has a little gas in the tank." Catching himself, he laughed out loud. "I don't doubt it for a minute. What do you have in mind?"

"Let's walk," said Emma. Taking his arm she led him outside. They strolled around the beautiful gardens before settling in the gazebo. She told Jon that she wanted to restore her corner of Springfield like what was happening in Riverside. To her surprise she learned that much of the area surrounding her block was not designated historically significant, thus not protected by the Historical Society guidelines.

Several years earlier, some of Jacksonville's older neighborhoods petitioned to be designated "historically important" and could therefore, be protected. The significance was important because it allowed homeowners access to special financial programs to do restoration on the old homes and buildings as well special tax status giving them even more financial incentives to buy, restore and/or live in those areas. Most of the restoration efforts had been centered on the neighborhoods north of Main Street. Emma's block and two other blocks were the only part of her section of Springfield under the historical designation. The other eight blocks around her were not, meaning the property owners could do anything they wanted to the homes, even raze them. Fortunately, their neglect had protected the structures to some extent. Many of the homes in Springfield were once some of the nicest in Jacksonville. This part of the city survived the great fire of the early 1900's. It wasn't until the late 1940's that people started migrating to suburbs and abandoning city life altogether. Many of the magnificent homes still stood, but had been ravaged by time and neglect. Segmented into multiplexes and mostly populated by lower income people not having the means to keep up the properties, many were in bad shape. Still, when Emma looked at the neighborhood she remembered what the area was once like and longed for it to be that way again.

"It looks like the first step is to get the rest of my little corner designated as historically significant," said Emma.

"That's an excellent first step and I know just the person to contact first. Councilwoman Sonya Danfora is your representative. She was extremely helpful in getting the other blocks protected under the historical umbrella. I'll start looking up the names of the property owners and compile a list. If we can get enough to agree, we can move on and try to get the historical designation ball rolling."

"Perfect. In the meantime, Cathy and I are planning to host a party here in a few weeks to raise awareness. Get me that list as soon as possible as well as the names of anyone else you think would be beneficial to our cause."

Jon cleared his throat. "Are you going to invite your favorite Mayor to this little shin-dig?" Emma rolled her eyes. "Absolutely! It's about time he does something useful for the community."

"This little get together could be very entertaining. I might even get a chance to play referee," Jon said.

It was no secret that Emma and the current Mayor didn't care much for each other. In some ways, because of Emma's family heritage, she was considered a kind of Jacksonville royalty. In her younger days she was active in several volunteer organizations and had a knack for raising money. She often used her home for such events. As time passed and old age set in, she became more restricted in her activities. For nearly a decade she'd kept to herself only occasionally leaving her home for medical reasons. But when she did leave, she was always so disappointed by the state of the neighborhood. Sometimes so much so that she'd call the Mayor and complain. She insisted he do something about the blight and clean out the riff-raff. On numerous occasions she tore into him accusing him of favoring big developers and neglecting the inner city neighborhoods. Often the calls ended with him hanging up on her. Jon remembered Emma's past fund raising efforts and contributions and was delighted to see her get involved again. He also felt a little sorry for the Mayor and any politician that dared do the political "two step" with her.

Chapter
7

Two weeks later Emma and Cathy hosted a lavish luncheon. It was a beautiful day - one could not have asked for better weather. Because of the size of the event, off-duty police officers helped with traffic and parking. A small army of caterers and other support staff had also been hired. Tables and tents were set up all round the garden. The house was open to her guests, but she wanted to take advantage of the property and host the party outside, weather permitting. And permitting it did!

Thomas did not disappoint. The new plantings, freshly cut grass, and perfectly manicured grounds completed the impressive home. The guests enjoyed themselves as they strolled in the beautiful gardens, occasionally stopping at the drink tables spread throughout the property to have dashingly handsome bartenders refresh their drinks. Emma wanted everyone to enjoy themselves and from her many years of hosting such events, she knew free booze went a long way in helping achieve this goal.

Jon and Emma carefully compiled a guest list made up of the who's who of Jacksonville's social elite along with any relevant political officials. Emma made it a point to invite all of the Springfield Historical Society board members as well as members from the citizens' group. And of course, the Mayor. She and Jon covered as many bases as possible.

Emma, Cathy, and Jon, stood on the front porch greeting guests as they arrived. Jon nudged Emma when he spotted the Mayor, John Douglas Jr., walking up the driveway. "Here comes your buddy, be nice."

"Emma! It's always nice to see you. You look well," the Mayor said as he inadvertently looked her up and down. His surprise was obvious. The last time he saw her publically she looked frail and sickly. But, today she stood proud, welcoming guests into her home with pride and confidence.

"And you, Mr. Mayor. It's nice you could join us for our little function. I hope we can count on your support."

"You know I'm always just a phone call away," he said with a wink and a smile.

She smiled back with the best fake smile she could manage and directed him into her home.

"I'm impressed," Cathy said. "I didn't think you'd let that one slip by." Jon chuckled and cleared his throat.

"He's still a prick, but today it's all about strategy," she said between clenched teeth as she smiled and greeted the next guest.

A few minutes later an elegantly dressed, beautiful woman in her 30s ascended the porch steps.

"Councilwoman Danfora. It's always nice to see you," said Jon. He stepped forward and shook her hand. "Allow me to introduce you to our generous host as well as one of your more cantankerous constituents, Mrs. Emma Perkins. Emma, this is the honorable Councilwoman Sonya Danfora."

Emma playfully slapped Jon on his arm. "Pay no attention to him. I'm not as bad as people say," she said extending her hand to the councilwoman.

She laughed and rolled her eyes at Jon. "It's an honor to finally make your acquaintance Mrs. Perkins. I've always had the deepest respect for you and your family," Councilwoman Danfora said. "You clearly have the most beautiful house and block in all of Springfield."

"Thank you and please call me Emma. I'd been meaning to call and congratulate you on your victory in the last election. It's so refreshing to have someone like you on the city council."

"Watch out Councilwoman. She's attempting to butter you up," Jon joked.

"You know very well that I don't ask for favors until after I've gotten my guests good and drunk," Emma said winking at the councilwoman.

"Well, if that's the case, I'd better go find a drink," said the Councilwoman.

"And after you do, please join me at my table for lunch," Emma said.

"I'm honored," she replied.

"Hubba, hubba," Cathy said under her breath as a strikingly attractive man ascended the steps with a beautiful woman on his arm.

"Ah, Mr. Ross, it's so nice of you and your lovely wife to join us today. Allow me to make the introductions," Jon said.

"No need," he replied. He extended his hand to Emma. "I know who Emma Carson Perkins is. It's delightful to finally meet you in person. I'm Devan Ross and this is my wife, Linda."

"Mr. Ross, it's nice to meet you. Jon tells me of all the great things you've done for our city, especially San Marco and Riverside. He says you've been especially generous in helping young people and small business."

Humbled, Devan bowed his head. "I've been fortunate in a variety of business ventures and feel it's my duty to give back to the community." He changed the subject. "We have something else in common, also."

Intrigued, Emma raised her eyebrows.

"We're both locals. Both born and raised in Jacksonville. The rare few."

Emma smiled wide nodding her head in agreement. "Not many of us left. We need to stick together," she said. "Well, then, fellow local, it's a pleasure to meet you and invite you into my home. I'd be honored to have you and your beautiful wife join me at my table for lunch."

"The honor is ours," Devan said.

"Damn," Cathy said under her breath as Devan and Linda walked through the front door. "Is it getting warm out here or is it just me?"

"Cathy, I'm shocked. I didn't think you had any hormones left," said Emma.

Frowning then smiling, Cathy said, "I can still look."

"Now, now, ladies, there's a lot more to Mr. Ross than good looks. He's definitely one you want to have in your corner. He has an uncanny way of getting things done.

"You mean he knows how to cut through red tape?" Emma asked.

"What red tape?"

"Interesting."

Making her way up the front porch stairs a woman could barely contain her excitement. "Mrs. Perkins, it's such an honor to be invited to your beautiful home."

"Emma, this is Angie Smith. She's the current president of the Springfield Historical Society," said Jon.

"Please, call me Emma. It's very nice to meet you, Mrs. Smith. I'd be honored if you would join me at my table at lunch. I want to bend your ear about a few things."

"I'd be delighted and please call me Angie."

Angie Smith was widely known for her calm and reserved manner. Her excitement over meeting Emma was clearly out of character.

Mrs. Smith and a select group of others had been meticulously chosen ahead of time to lunch at Emma's table. She and Jon had prepared a short list of key players she wanted to make sure got special attention.

"Ok, that about does it. Hopefully most of our guests are all boozed up and feeling good by now. Should we get this show on the road?" Emma asked. She gestured for the others to enter the house. It was 12:30pm. Time for the garden party lunch to start.

As they entered the house a sloppily dressed, short pudgy man with the worst comb over ever rushed up the steps. "Sorry I'm late. I was held up in traffic. William Pollock."

"No need to rush Councilman. I'm sure you won't be the only late arrival," Emma said extending her hand to greet him while trying not to be repulsed by the strong smell of alcohol on his breath.

"Councilman Pollock represents the blocks just outside your district, literally right across the street," Jon said. He also smelled the strong aroma and wanted to diffuse the situation before Emma made an unflattering comment.

"Is that so?" Emma asked. Her attitude shifted to greeting him warmly despite her reservations. "Welcome. It's an honor to have you in my home. We have much to talk about. Please, join me at my table for lunch."

"I'd be delighted, ma'am. Thank you."

She directed him through the house and into the backyard where the lunch was about to start.

"Wow! I think he's already drunk his lunch for the day," Cathy said.

"He's one of our allies?" Emma asked Jon. "Do you think we can count on him?"

"He's a pretty small fish as far as the city council is concerned, but right now he has something we want so he's just as important as any of the other players in this game," Jon said.

Taking both by the arm Emma led them out into the backyard. "No worries guys. I'm a Navy girl and he's not the first drunk I've come across. Let's do this."

Chapter
8

A large tent was set up behind the house for the luncheon. Tables and chairs had been beautifully prepared. Emma spared no expense in creating the elegant atmosphere of a garden party from a bygone era. Escorted by Cathy and Jon, Emma walked over to a small stage where she took a microphone and requested for her guests to take their seats.

"Ladies and gentlemen, I welcome all of you to my home on this beautiful spring afternoon. I'm so pleased to see so many in attendance. But, I'll admit, this is somewhat self-serving on my part. As you may have noticed driving in, my little section of Springfield is desperately in need of help. Homes are falling apart, businesses are abandoned, and the residents who do live here wrestle daily to make ends meet. This was once a thriving area of Jacksonville. Trust me, I know, I was here! Wow! That really dates me."

The crowd laughed.

"I know progress is being made around town in helping restore and bring back many long neglected neighborhoods. Even here in Springfield, change is coming. Still, your support is needed to continue the process. With the exception of my block and the two on either side to the east and west, everything to the south is not protected under the historical preservation umbrella. Once beautiful homes are deteriorating and being torn down. With the protection of a historical designation, people can get financial help to preserve and restore these houses and buildings. Still, I'm not one to force things down other people's throats. This has to be the choice of the neighborhoods and those living in and representing them. I invited all of you here today to open a dialogue so we can start discussing the possibility of getting a historical designation for the surrounding areas. I want all of us to work together to explore the positives and negatives before making any decisions. But most importantly, I want to shine a light on this long-neglected neighborhood and, hopefully, work together in restoring and rebuilding this section of town by whatever means. It once proudly represented the center of Jacksonville. With all our help, we can see it restored to such a position before I leave this earth. And just so you know, I'm 86, so we need to get moving. Thank you all for coming. Enjoy your lunch."

The guests erupted into applause as Emma was escorted from the stage to her table where her special guests were on their feet and continued applauding before sitting down to lunch.

The conversations around the table ranged widely. Many focused on Springfield and what a historical designation would do for the areas around Emma's block. Most believed her home would make a beautiful centerpiece to the preservation efforts north and south of Main Street.

Emma's table was the biggest under the tent and round so all parties could see and hear each other. Emma had Cathy to her left and Jon to her right, but this did little to stop Angie Smith from sharing her overly enthusiastic ideas with Emma and the entire table. The Mayor was seated next to Angie with his wife on his other side. Councilwoman Danfora who represented Emma's block and most of Springfield was next to the mayor. Devan and Linda were next putting them directly across from Emma. Councilman Pollock was next to Devan's wife. Smelling the alcohol, Devan changed seats with Linda. Pollock was noticeably nervous when Devan did this.

"So Mr. Pollock, this is potentially good news for you and your district. With a historical designation, residents and small business owners will have access to loans and be able to make major improvements," Devan said. He directed his conversation in a manner where everyone heard him. He put his hand on Pollock's shoulder in a congratulatory gesture, but what the other guests did not see was how hard he was squeezing it. Devan was not happy that he would show up drunk to this event. It was a clear sign of disrespect to their host.

Sucking up the pain, Pollock gasped with relief when Devan let go. "Yes, this could be good news for my constituents in the long run. Investment the area could sure use." Pollock was nervous while trying to appear and sound enthusiastic.

"Well, congratulations then. And let me be the first to say that I look forward working with you and your constituents in helping achieve Mrs. Perkins' dream." Devan looked him squarely in the eye. But it wasn't a look of congratulations, it was a warning. And Pollock got the message.

Emma noticed the body language. She didn't know much about Mr. Ross, but she liked what she saw so far.

On the other side of Pollock was Daniel Webster. He was the head of the citizens group representing historical Springfield. He and Angie worked together to keep the residents involved and committed to the restoration of the area. They could also organize a considerable block of vocal residents when needed to get the city's attention.

"I'd like to offer a toast to our gracious host and thank her for this wonderful lunch. On a personal note, I want you to know that I'll try to do everything in my power to help bring these forgotten blocks and residents and residences into the historical fold. Thank you Mrs. Perkins," Daniel said, raising his glass.

"Wait! I have something to add," the mayor said hastily. He stood up from his chair. "Emma, I know we don't always see eye to eye on things but I have to thank you for your devotion and commitment to your area. You never gave up. I truly hope we can accomplish your goal and bring back the Springfield you once knew. Thank you, Emma!"

With that, everyone cheered and drank a toast to Emma and Springfield.

# # #

Thomas and Tor could hear the garden party from inside the cottage. Emma and Cathy wanted him to join the festivities, but Thomas politely declined. He didn't like large crowds. Instead, he opted to hang out with Tor in the cottage. "Sounds like Miss Emma and Miss Cathy are having a nice party. Should be some good leftovers for us later, Mr. Tor." Thomas played with his toys on the living room floor. Tor looked on from his usual position in a chair. Occasionally, Tor would cock his head and listen when hearing music from the luncheon, but otherwise was uninterested in what was going on outside. He enjoyed being with Thomas no matter what the activity. Content, he periodically bathed himself as he watched Thomas play from his vantage point in the chair.

Chapter
9

The following day, Emma and Jon met for lunch to discuss the benefits gained from the garden party as well as plan their next move.

"Overall, I think it was a huge success, Emma. Now you have a good feel for who the major players are. I think our next move should be to compile a list of positive and negative consequences of gaining the historical designation. A good number of the residents and business owners in attendance seemed interested in the idea, but requested more information."

"Agreed. Most people I talked with were concerned about being burdened by the restrictions that would be imposed on them which is the downside of the designation. Some of them could be costly to people on a fixed or limited income."

"But the upside is they're also eligible for construction and rehab grants, loans, tax breaks, and more," said Jon.

"True. But for now, I think the best thing for us to do is put all our cards on the table. Be as honest and upfront as we can. Fortunately, my block and the ones immediately adjacent to me are already under the historical umbrella. It's the other eight we need to worry about. That rundown warehouse complex to the West now sits where some beautiful homes once stood. I want to prevent anything like that from ever happening to any of the remaining blocks." She looked west in the direction of the complex and frowned before continuing. "But for now, I think our best weapon is information. We need to get all the property and business owners better informed and educated about both sides of the equation then convince them this is the right move for everyone." She smiled a cunning smile and nodded at Jon.

"Emma, I can't tell you how good it is to have you back. It's been dull as hell around here without you." He gently squeezed her hand. "I'll call Councilwoman Danfora and see what she can do to help us. The blocks in question aren't technically in her district, but she's been good to the residents and business owners she does represent. You're fortunate to be under her jurisdiction."

"I agree. It was a pleasure talking with Councilwoman Danfora. To your point, she told me she had considerable experience working within the historical guidelines and looked forward to helping in any way she could." Pausing for a second, Emma shrugged and then sighed. "It's too bad she can't annex the eight blocks in question into her district. I wasn't impressed with Pollock."

Jon shook his head and sat up in his chair at the mere mention of his name.

"He's a complete slob. And, he was drunk! Can you believe that? How unprofessional," Emma said. She was fidgety. "My father would've set him straight right then and there. I was about to!"

Jon tried to stifle a chuckle while motioning for her to relax with his hands. "That's why I intervened. We may not like it, but he's an important player - one you need in your corner. At least for now."

"Be that as it may, next time I may not be so restrained." Thinking for a minute Emma herself chuckled. Then she was contemplative.

"What's going through that head of yours?" Jon asked.

"I was just thinking about Mr. Ross. Call me crazy but, Pollock seemed down right terrified of the man. I was amused by their interaction. What's his story?"

"Ah yes, the mysterious Mr. Ross. You want him in your corner." Jon sat up in his chair with a sly smile before leaning in closer. "And no, you're not crazy at all. To be honest, I love having him at functions involving our city's movers and shakers. Watching city leaders and other pillars of the community stumble and shake in their shoes in his presence is always entertaining," he said.

This intrigued Emma. She noticed Pollock's nervous demeanor when Mr. Ross spoke to him. She also noticed his fear. "Oh Jon, you know how an old woman likes her gossip. I think there's a good story here. Besides being dashingly handsome, what's his deal and how can he help us?"

"Mr. Devan Ross, like you, is a local. He was born and raised in Jacksonville. He and his partners ran several small businesses. The Gallery of San Marco is one of his most notable. He gained some local notoriety when he sponsored several student arts programs. But the real story had to do with events surrounding a club he owns. Nothing's been verified, but the gossip is interesting none the less."

Cathy walked out onto the porch where they were having lunch to check on them and see if they needed anything.

"You're just in time. Jon was about to tell me some juicy gossip about your handsome Mr. Ross," Emma said.

"Do tell," Cathy said. She was smiling from ear to ear as she pulled up a chair and sat next to Emma.

"Okay Ladies, cool your jets. The story goes something like this. Apparently he was in the process of buying the building his club now occupies when he was double crossed by some city officials and a certain prominent religious organization."

Emma crossed her arms. "Him too, huh?"

Nodding, Jon continued. "It's not confirmed, but rumor has it he organized a meeting at his lawyer's office where several of our more prominent officials were present. Some say they weren't given a choice. No nobody outside that meeting knows exactly what happened, but one thing's for sure, Mr. Ross got his club."

The ladies exchanged sly looks. "Wouldn't you liked to have been a fly on the wall that day?" Cathy asked.

"From that day on, his construction company has had the most uncanny way of cutting through red tape. So much so, that it's now the most successful and highly sought after construction business in Northeast Florida. And if that wasn't enough, Ross also appears to have extraordinary luck when it came to other business ventures. People and other companies want him involved in their projects. Nobody knew what happened in that meeting all those years ago but, whatever it was, it's still in effect to this day.

The ladies sat quietly for a few seconds reflecting on what he told them.

Breaking the silence, Jon continued, "As I said, having him at functions where political officials or other prominent citizens are present is always entertaining. You saw it for yourself. Still, since he got married a few years ago, he's kind of slowed down. He travels a lot with his wife and friends. You might be familiar with one of his friends, the famous author, Rachel Winters?"

Cathy jumped when she heard the name "Oh yes, I'm a huge fan of hers. I love her work!" Cathy looked over at Emma "You really need to suck up to the handsome Mr. Ross. Let's have him over for dinner! I want to meet Miss Winters."

Amused by Cathy, Emma patted her leg. "Calm down, woman. First things first. My word, you're about as excited as a groupie school girl."

"That's not a bad idea," Jon said. "He already knows who you are. I'll admit, I put him on your guest list to shake things up some, but maybe you should have him over to talk business? Restoration?" It would be a good opportunity for the two of you to get better acquainted. He's been a huge supporter of restoration and preservation in San Marco, Riverside and Avondale.

"I get what you're saying, but can we trust him? How do we know he won't swoop in and buy up those blocks then build tacky condos or something?" Emma asked.

"I don't think you need to worry about that. If anything, he's pretty serious about preservation and restoration. That's actually how his construction business started. He and his partners rehabbed older homes. I'm telling you Emma, him in your corner gives you leverage."

Emma looked at Cathy who was nodding excitedly.

Jon narrowed his eyes as he smiled at Emma. "One other thing. He's not a big fan of your favorite mayor or his corrupt family either."

Emma's face lit up as she patted the table approvingly. "Well, then. That does it. We'll invite Mr. Ross and his lovely wife to have dinner with us. All of us," she said to Jon, "You can help me sell him on our cause. Let's introduce him to my little corner of Springfield and try to impress upon him the importance of preserving the area, historical designation or not."

"Sounds good. Just tell me when and I'll make the arrangements," Jon said as he stood to leave.

"I need to get a new dress," said Cathy pretending to fan herself. Emma rolled her eyes and looked at Jon. "She doesn't have a chance."

Chapter
10

Tor proved to be a vicious hunter. It wasn't uncommon for Thomas to find "gifts" from Tor on his doorstep in the morning. Rats, mice, and moles were his usual victims. The occasional snake and lizard added some variety to the mix. After Tor caught and killed the mole in the garden, Thomas was impressed. But as the weeks passed, the number of kills Tor was racking up alarmed him. Thomas had the mind of a child, and even though rats and mice were nuisance animals, they were still living things and this began to bother him. He expressed his concerns to Emma and Cathy one night at dinner.

"You have to understand Thomas this is what cats do. Tor likes you. Killing and leaving things on your front stoop is his way of showing you how much," Cathy said as she tried to comfort Thomas and ease his concerns.

"Maybe he feels it's his way of earning his keep," Emma said. She tried to lighten the conversation. Tor was sitting next to her on the bench purring loudly as she scratched him behind his ears.

Thomas thought about it for a moment. "I like Mr. Tor. He's my friend. I just wish he didn't kill so much."

# # #

A few days later Thomas awoke and started his day as he usually did. When he opened his front door, he was stopped dead in his tracks. Looking down at the doormat he froze in place.

"Mr. Tor, no…what have you done?"

# # #

"Where is Thomas this morning?" Emma asked. She dumped a load of bacon on a plate and looked out the kitchen window in the direction of the path leading to the cottage. Tor was purring as he sat on his usual bench eyeing the bacon. He knew he'd get some after everyone was seated.

"Strange. It's not like Thomas to be late for breakfast." Cathy said. She opened the kitchen door and stepped out onto the porch.

"Go see what's keeping him will you, dear? I'll finish getting breakfast together," Emma said and motioned for her to go. "And take this rascal with you. I'm afraid if I turn my back he's going to eat all the bacon." Emma looked right at Tor.

"Come on, boy. Let's go see what's keeping Thomas." Cathy pointed toward the open kitchen door. Tor jumped down enthusiastically and followed Cathy out.

Not that long ago, Cathy would have never left Emma to such a task alone, but these days, she knew better than to argue. Every day, Cathy was amazed with the increased level of mobility and independence Emma presented. Prior to Tor's arrival, Emma was completely dependent on Cathy for everything. Now, she rarely needed or asked for help. If anything, Emma was assisting Cathy more. Cathy hadn't missed that Emma's health improved after Tor moved in. She wondered if there was a connection. From the first day he showed up, she noticed that Tor and Emma bonded. He meant a lot to her and her to him. Cathy especially liked that Tor and Thomas had become good friends. Other than Emma and herself, Thomas had limited opportunities for social interaction with others. Even though Tor was a cat, Thomas treated him like a person and made it a point to explain things to him as if he could understand. Emma and Cathy noticed how much Tor had helped bring Thomas out of his shell. As she walked, Cathy looked down at Tor and thought maybe he was somehow casting a magic spell over all of them.

###

The long, winding path to Thomas's cottage was bordered by dense vegetation. This was on purpose. The original intent was to hide the small cottage so it wouldn't be seen and spoil the view of the grounds. However, over the years, Thomas had fixed up the cottage and it now made a beautiful addition to the property. He built a small stone patio with a rock retaining wall running around the edge as well as a kidney shaped pond and cascading rock waterfall next to it. It was his favorite spot on the whole property. He enjoyed sitting outside listening to the water and looking at his favorite picture books. Thomas liked the seclusion. Nestled under the shade of a large live oak, the cottage itself was surrounded by huge azaleas and other vegetation allowed to grow wild. Looking at Thomas's corner of the property from the main house, it looked like a small well-kept forest. No one would ever know a house was hidden in the overgrown corner.

As Cathy rounded the last corner she abruptly stopped when she saw Thomas sitting in a chair on his patio holding something in his hand. He was slowly rocking back and forth and mumbling in a low voice. She could tell something was very wrong. "Thomas, honey, is everything ok?"

He looked up at her with tears in his eyes. "Look what Mr. Tor did," he said. He gently held a dead blue bird in his large hands. "Mr. Tor killed a bird..." his voice trailed off to a muffled whimper.

"Oh, Thomas. I'm so sorry. But, you know how Tor is. He's a cat. It's what he does. I'm sure he didn't do it to hurt you."

"I know Miss Cathy, but my mom told me birds were like angels. My mom said when she died she hoped she'd come back as a blue bird, her favorite bird. Then, she could be free to fly anywhere she wanted and would be able to watch over me from high in the trees. Tor killed an angel Miss Cathy. God is going to be mad at Mr. Tor."

Seeing how upset Thomas was broke her heart. Cathy felt the tears welling in her eyes. She leaned down and hugged him with a warm embrace. "I had no idea your mother told you that about birds. It's so beautiful." She held him tightly for a little bit rocking him gently. She noticed Tor sitting on the edge of the patio observing them both. He almost looked like he was listening. Could he understand what they were talking about? Did he know how much killing the bird hurt Thomas? It almost appeared as if he did. Cathy thought he looked remorseful if that was even possible.

"And don't worry about Tor. I don't think God will be too mad at him. He knows how cats are. And Tor didn't know. He's just a cat." Cathy pointed to Tor who had kept his distance. "No more killing birds, Mister. Do I make myself clear? Thomas doesn't like it, and quite frankly, neither do I."

Tor slowly walked over to them with his head lowered. When he was within an arm's reach he stopped and looked up wide-eyed and meowed quietly. Cathy couldn't believe what she was seeing. It was as if he had understood what she said to him. "I think he's trying to apologize to you Thomas."

Thomas looked down at him. "Please don't kill anymore birds Mr. Tor. Birds are angels. They're here to watch over us and protect us." A tear ran down his cheek as he spoke. Tor lowered his head again. Cathy couldn't believe what she was seeing. She'd have sworn Tor understood what Thomas said. "No more killing Mr. Tor," he said again as he reached down to pet him. Tor immediately started purring and rubbed against his legs.

"How about we all go have some breakfast and then later we'll find a nice place in the garden to bury the bird," Cathy said trying to lighten the mood.

After breakfast, Thomas, Emma, Cathy and Tor held a small funeral for the bird next to the cottage. Later that morning Cathy gave Emma a more detailed accounting of the incident.

"Call me crazy, but I could have sworn Tor understood everything we were saying. And the way he approached Thomas was as if he was apologizing." She sat next to Emma on the porch enjoying the crisp morning air. They could see Thomas and Tor in the yard. Thomas was weeding and Tor was lying in the grass not far from him.

"Sometimes I feel like Tor understands me, too," Emma said. "He's so attentive, at times I feel like he's looking out for me, protecting me in a way. He's a unique cat, that's for sure. We're fortunate to have him in our lives. I just hope he understood what you said to him for all our sakes." Emma was use to making tough decisions and knew if Tor kept killing birds she might be forced to find him another home. The emotional impact on Thomas was her primary concern.

She cleared her throat. "I had no idea his mother told him that about birds but I can definitely see her saying it. His mother was such a beautiful woman."

That night, as Tor lay curled next to Emma on her bed, she lowered her book. "Thanks for coming into our lives boy. But please do me a favor and don't kill anymore birds. Thomas is very special to me and I don't like seeing him upset." She reached over and gently pet him. As she did, his purring became louder. Emma smiled. "I know you understand every word I'm saying. Good night, boy." She turned off the light and soon drifted off into a deep restful sleep.

# # #

The next night after Thomas let Tor out, he walked up the path in the direction of the house, but instead of going to the oak tree and climbing up to Emma's open window, he headed down the driveway toward the main gates. He walked along the wall for a short distance until he found what he was looking for. Behind the bushes was a gap - the exact spot where he entered the property the day he was escaping from the animal control officers months ago. It was only 9:00pm, but darkness had fallen. He hesitated at the opening for a moment and peered out. Satisfying himself that there was no danger, he set out into the mostly deserted neighborhood. He was on a mission.

Sticking to the shadows, Tor quietly moved between the alleys and buildings unseen. He knew the area well having lived on the streets for some time before being chased into Emma's secret sanctuary. These were familiar hunting grounds.

Several blocks from Emma's house was an industrial warehouse complex. Beautiful homes once occupied these blocks, but now, little was left to indicate a thriving residential community once existed there. Not having a historical designation, there was nothing to protect these blocks from the wrecking ball. This was Tor's territory and stretched for many blocks in all directions. Though he was a formidable hunter in his own right, the area was not without its dangers. People, vehicles, busy streets, and packs of wild dogs were an ever present danger. But, Tor knew his way around and knew how to avoid the more dangerous sections.

30 minutes later, he arrived at his destination. On the corner of one of the warehouse blocks was a sandwich shop that had been there for decades. Closed for the evening, the dumpster in the side ally was teeming with night life. Tor quietly approached being careful to remain unseen. His dark coat and white markings helped him blend into the shadows. Rats and mice were frequent visitors to the dumpster. Lured by the garbage thrown out earlier in the day, Tor knew it was just a matter of time before they came calling. Hidden in the shadows, he waited. The only sound was the dull thumping of music coming from a band practicing in one of the nearby warehouses. Motionless. He didn't have to wait long. Noticing movement by the corner of the building, his eyes locked on to it. It was a large rat. His instincts were heightened. Quietly he approached using shadows and other debris in ally as cover. Unaware of the predator lurking in the darkness, the rat ran down the edge of the building toward the dumpster. Pausing next to a box to sniff the air, the rat hesitated. Smelling something on the wind, the rat froze in place, but it was too late. Before he had time to retreat, Tor leapt from behind a nearby box and pounced on the rat. With one swift motion Tor clamped his jaws around the rat's neck. A faint shrill could be heard before going silent. As the life drained from the small animal, Tor's eyes

glowed bright yellow. For the next couple hours Tor repeated his ambush technique multiple times before heading home.

# # #

It was 11:30pm and Emma was getting worried. Tor usually made his way to her room by now. Standing at the window, Emma strained to look out into the yard. Seeing something moving below, she felt a huge since of relief when she saw Tor emerge from the shadows and approach the tree. With his usual grace, he climbed up and within seconds was standing on the roof purring loudly as Emma affectionately embraced him.

"I was getting worried about you, Mister. Better late than never. Come in. I was just about to call it a night." Emma's relief surprised her. She realized she was a lot more worried about Tor than she cared to admit. After doing his nightly routine of exploring her room, Tor jumped up on the bed and assumed his position. Emma wondered what took him so long to show up but didn't dwell on it. It had been a long day and she was ready go to sleep.

# # #

Tor's nocturnal habits became fairly routine. After leaving the grounds, he carefully maneuvered through the neighborhoods eventually making his way to the sandwich shop and the alley behind it. Occasionally, he ventured out in different directions in search of new hunting grounds, but usually didn't stay too long. After satisfying his hunting needs, he would make his way back to Emma's by 11:00 or 11:30pm. This was instinctual of course, for he had no way of telling time. Emma adjusted to his later arrival and made it a point to wait for him each night.

Chapter
11

The Jaguar XK8 looked noticeably out of place as it entered the dark, gated parking lot in front of a large rundown warehouse building. It was one of the warehouses bordering the eight remaining residential neighborhood blocks Emma and the Historical Society were trying to protect. Prior to Emma, there had been several attempts by progressive-minded people to re-take the area by trying to renovate some of the beautiful century-old buildings, but the struggle had been difficult.

Coming to a stop next to three other vehicles, a young man in his late twenties got out of the car and stretched. It was a little past 9:00pm and he knew it was going to be a long night. But first, he had other business to attend to. He reached back into the car and retrieved a brown paper bag. Instead of joining his fellow bandmates in the warehouse, he walked toward an alley. "Here kitty, kitty, kitty, I've got something for you."

Hearing the Jaguar pull up, another young man came out of the warehouse. "What are you doing? Every time we come here to practice you try to get that cat to come to you. It ain't going to happen so you might as well give it up."

"I'm determined to win him over. I'll be in in a minute. I have to make my bi-weekly offering," the Jaguar driver responded holding up the paper bag.

Entering the alley, he spotted the cat sitting between two large wooden boxes. "Hey, buddy. You ready for some chow?" he asked. He shook the small paper bag and squatted down in an attempt to cox the cat toward him.

Looking out from between the two large wooden crates, the cat meowed softly acknowledging the familiar voice but kept a safe distance.

"When are you going to realize I'm not going to hurt you?" he asked trying to get the cat to come to him. "Okay, I see how it is. If you won't come to me then I'll come to you." Cautiously, he approached. The cat appeared anxious. "It's okay. Relax." He walked slowly in the cat's direction.

Nervous anticipation caused the cat to retreat into a gap between the crates then return and peak out. Not making eye contact, the young man got as close as he dared without frightening him away. Slowly, he opened the bag, hesitating for a second, he looked at the cat. "You know what I have?, Your favorite. Turkey meat. You hungry?" He spread some meat on the ground several feet away, forcing him to come out of his hiding place.

Safe between the crates, the cat meowed and stretched toward the pile of turkey as far as he could, but couldn't reach it. He quickly retreated back between the crates.

At this point the young man usually stood up and walked away but this time he was determined to pet the cat so he remained squatting by the pile of turkey. Confused, the cat tried to approach, but lost his nerve and retreated back. He did this several more times before going back into the gap and staying there.

"Okay, you win. I guess it won't be tonight." The young man was just about to stand up when the cat slowly slinked out and cautiously approached the turkey. The young man remained still. Stretching, the cat snatched a chunk of turkey and pulled back to eat it. He approached again and took another piece of meat. The last large chunk. Next time, he approached the pile he stayed.

"That's it, little buddy, relax. It's okay." Slowly the young man raised his hand and reached for the cat, but his movement caused him to pull back. He lowered his hand, but not all the way. When the cat returned to the pile of meat he tried it again. This time he was able to gently caress the cat's back.

"It's okay, buddy. Nobody is going to hurt you. You're a hungry fellow." Noticing a small brass name tag hanging from a black collar, he turned it so he could read it. The cat was so consumed by the turkey, he didn't seem to mind. Flipping it over, it had a single word on it, Tor, and an address.

"Tor. Is that your name?" he asked gently stroking the cats back and neck. Tor finished the turkey, but did not run off. Calmer, he purred loudly while rubbing against the man's legs enjoying the interaction. "Looks like you're a big softie after all." He continued scratching Tor's neck and body.

"You have a friend," said another man standing by the ally entrance.

"It looks that way."

"About time. You've been trying to befriend that cat since we started rehearsing here. How long has it been, a month?"

"Closer to three I think."

"Well, I hate to cut this bonding experience short, Ryan, but we have a lot of material to work through tonight so you might want to say goodbye to your new friend. James wants to work on those new songs we're adding to next week's performance plus get a good solid rehearsal in. Hope your voice is up to it, because it's looking like a long night."

"Relax, Allen. All work and no play will make you a dull boy," Ryan said.

"Yeah, whatever. Say goodnight to your little buddy and get in there before James has a stroke," Allen joked.

"Okay Tor, looks like I have to go to rehearsal. You stay safe and I'll see you in a few days."

Over the next several months, Tor became a frequent visitor on rehearsal nights, always greeting Ryan and the rest of the band sometimes even leaving them the gift of a dead rat to find later. The band members liked Tor and each made it a point to interact with him in some way. Even Allen who was allergic to cats. It wasn't uncommon to find Tor in the warehouse hanging out with the band members while they waited for the others to arrive. But, once the actual rehearsal begin, Tor usually called it a night. "Maybe he doesn't care much for our music," Allen said. They all laughed."

Chapter
12

Eyes barely open, a small kitten meowed quietly in the darkness but, heard no response from his mother or other siblings. Having aimlessly wandered far down a dark alley within the sprawling warehouse complex and away from the safety of the others, he waited for his mother to find him. It was not the first time this small kitten wandered away. It was becoming common for his mother to return to the nest and find him gone. Since his eyes opened, the young kitten had been venturing out exploring his blurry surroundings. Peering out from under the safety of a broken crate, the kitten meowed lightly again, but got no response. His new born eyes can't see the devastation just around the corner less than twenty feet away. Little did he know, but his wandering tendencies served him well this night. Eyes barely open, he kept crying with no response. Shivering and hungry, the small kitten waited alone in the darkness.

# # #

Having gotten an early start to evening, Tor ventured further out into the warehouse complex than usual in search of his nightly prey. He was driven not only by the instinct to hunt but also by a craving, a need he could only satisfy by taking the lives of smaller animals. Having encountered and killed two large rats and one mouse, he had successfully satisfied both needs this night. Feeling energized, he looked forward to getting home and curling up with Emma.

Attempting to save time, Tor opted for a more direct and less used side alley cutting through part of the dilapidated warehouse complex. Having been built in the early seventies, the complex had been widely used, but never well maintained. Now, only a handful of businesses rented space and occasionally a local band used one of the better buildings to practice. Emma knew the complex well. When she returned home to help see to the care of Thomas's mother, a local developer had just purchased the neglected blocks and was beginning the task of removing the many rundown homes. It saddened Emma to see this large section of Springfield erased from the city's history but she realized there wasn't anything she could do to stop it. Most of the residents had abandoned this section of Springfield over the years, leaving the blocks and structures to deteriorate over time.

Familiar with the warehouse complex grounds, Tor knew the area was dangerous since it was also frequented by packs of wild dogs. Moving cautiously down the dark alley, he suddenly stopped. Hearing a faint cry coming from somewhere ahead in the darkness, he approached with caution. When he rounded a sharp corner in the alley, the scent of blood and death overwhelmed him. Startled by the sight of a mutilated female cat, he could still smell the strong odor of dog in the air. As he approached, he found the remains of two small kittens that had also been mauled by the dogs. His senses were heightened. Though he was a large cat he knew he was no match for a pack of wild dogs. Hearing the faint cry again, Tor followed the sound to a broken crate. Sensing a presence, the kitten stumbled out on unsteady legs expecting to be greeted by his mother. Instead, Tor stood there studying the small animal. The kitten nuzzled Tor expecting to be picked up and carried back to the safety of the others. Hearing dogs barking in the distance, Tor made a command decision to take the kitten with him. He knew the area was unsafe and needed to get himself and the kitten back to the safety of Emma's house. Gently picking him up by his neck, Tor hurriedly made his way home. When he got to the compound, he knew he couldn't carry the kitten up to Emma's bedroom so he took it to the patio outside Thomas's cottage. Knowing it still wasn't safe, Tor hopped into his favorite patio chair and curled up with the small kitten nestled safely next to him. Soon, both drifted off to sleep.

# # #

It was well past 1:00am as Emma stood at her bedroom window straining to look out into the darkness.

"Where are you Tor?" she asked more than once as she paced her room worrying that something might have happened to him. It wasn't like Tor not to show up. Every night for months he'd made his way to her and spent the night on her bed. Finally deciding to turn in, she left the window open in the hope he would soon arrive.

# # #

As usual Thomas was the first to wake up. After getting dressed and making his bed he opened the front door. Always looking down in case Tor decided to leave him a gift, Thomas was again stopped dead in his tracks. Tor stood there meowing loudly with a small kitten on the mat next to him also crying out.

"Mr. Tor, where did he come from?" Thomas asked, squatting down to look at Tor's young friend. "Why he's just a baby, Mr. Tor. We need to take him to Miss Cathy and Mrs. Emma right away. Thomas scooped him up gently in his large hands and quickly made his way to the main house.

# # #

When Emma awoke she noticed right away that she felt tired. Looking around she still saw no sign of Tor. Slowly, she got out of bed and began her morning routine. Much slower, Emma still managed to get dressed. She also felt weak; like her energy of the past many months was greatly reduced. Figuring it was because she stayed up so late waiting for Tor she tried to shake the feeling, but still had to move with considerably more caution as she made her way down stairs.

Making her way down the long hall to join the others, Emma could hear the commotion in the kitchen. Cathy and Thomas were fussing over something on the table. When she realized what it was she broke into a huge smile. "A kitten! Where did that come from?" Emma asked. She made her way to the table to join the group.

"What's wrong with you this morning? You're moving like an old lady," Cathy asked.

Emma waved her off. "I didn't sleep well last night. I stayed up worrying about Tor. He never showed up."

"He's there waiting for you," Cathy said pointing to the bench seat.

Reaching out to pat his head, Emma felt a huge since of relief seeing him there. Tor immediately hopped down and started rubbing against her legs purring excitedly. She sat down on the bench.

"Where were you last night, boy? I missed you." Tor resumed his position on the bench and sat next to Emma still purring. He nuzzled against her side happy to be with her.

"You're like two peas in a pod," Cathy said. "Let's eat and then we need to get some formula for this poor little guy. Looks like we might have a new member of the family."

"Where did he come from?" Emma asked.

Thomas excitedly piped up, "When I opened my door this morning, Mr. Tor was standing on my door mat with his friend."

"Well, aren't you just full of surprises, Mister?" Emma said looking at Tor.

They found a box and lined it with a soft towel.

"That'll do for now. I'm sure he's hungry so I'll give him a bath then feed him after we pick up some formula," Cathy said. She gently placed him in the box. Cathy, Emma, and Thomas looked at their little guest happy to have the new addition to the family.

After breakfast, Cathy and Thomas went to the store for formula and to do the other weekly shopping. Emma reminded them that they were hosting Mr. Ross and his wife for dinner in two days and had them pick up a few extra things for the evening. Having accepted Emma's dinner invitation, the ladies were looking forward to Devan's visit.

Still feeling tired, Emma checked on the kitten one more time before returning to her room to lie down for a bit. A few minutes later she felt a thud on the bed and opened her eyes to find Tor standing there.

"Ah, there you are, boy. I'm exhausted today because of you," she teased. Reaching out, she patted him on the back. Tor laid down and stretched out like a sphinx facing her. "I stayed up well past my bedtime waiting on you. Still, I guess you had a good reason. I don't know what the story is with that kitten, but I'm guessing something must have happened to his mother for you to bring him here. Good move my friend. We'll take good care of him," she said lightly stroking his head. Feeling her eyes getting heavy she gave in and drifted off to sleep.

Tor sat watching Emma for a few minutes. He could see her chest moving and hear her shallow light breathing. He looked on, almost as if he was evaluating her, studying her stillness. Satisfying himself that she was sleeping soundly, he walked up the bed. Hesitating, he gently placed one paw on her chest and leaned in close to her face. His breathing and hers synced like they were one. Leaning in closer, his eyes began to glow a brilliant yellow green. Emma's breathing began to change. Every breath she took was a little deeper than the last. With each breath, Tor's eyes glowed a little less. He leaned in close to her face, noses almost touching. After about a minute, Tor shut his eyes and extinguished the glow. He slowly stepped back off of Emma and then assumed his normal position curled up next to her on the bed. Soon, he too drifted off to sleep.

# # #

Two hours later Emma was awakened by Cathy calling out from the kitchen. "We're home," she shouted as she and Thomas entered with arms full of groceries.

Hearing her, Emma's eyes fluttered open. She looked down and saw Tor laying on his back stretched out across the bed. Chuckling and shaking her head, Emma sat up effortlessly and tried get out of the bed without waking him up. But unknown to her, Tor was watching through barely open eyes. She noticed how much better she felt. "Wow, I must have really needed that nap." She stood and stretched. Feeling steady on her feet she headed down stairs to help Cathy and Thomas. Tor watched as she left the room then drifted off to sleep.

After bathing the kitten and preparing the formula, Cathy sat Thomas down and showed him how to feed him with the small formula bottle. Nervous at first, Thomas soon got the hang of it. After a few minutes, he was a natural.

"So what are we going to name the poor little guy?" Emma asked.

"I guess we do need to come up with a name for the poor thing," Cathy said looking at Thomas. "Do you have any ideas?"

"How about Poe? Like Poe little guy?" Thomas joked.

Not having the heart to correct him, Cathy and Emma looked at each other and shrugged.

"Poe it is then," Emma said. "I like that name, short and simple. Welcome to the family little one."

Chapter
13

Not wanting to arrive at Emma's for dinner too early, Devan and Linda killed time driving through the streets of Springfield taking in the sights. It had been several years since he'd spent any time in this part of the city.

"I'd forgotten how beautiful these old houses are," Devan said. Fortunately, some progress was being made preserving and restoring some of the homes and buildings spread throughout the area. As they continued through the streets, they were impressed. Devan and Linda both enjoyed and appreciated the different styles and architecture.

"Such a beautiful neighborhood. Even the homes not restored are impressive. You don't find this level of craftsmanship in newer developments," Linda said with genuine admiration. "Just look at all the detail." She was pointing out the window at a grand, but rundown, Victorian.

"I agree. Even the badly neglected homes still exude a sense of grandeur," Devan said. He slowed to look at the huge, unrestored Victorian house Linda pointed to. Even though much work still needed to be done to bring the area back to its full potential, they were pleased with the progress made so far. It was clear that the people who had the means took great pride in their homes.

When they reached Emma's house, the large gates were left open. Devan drove up the driveway and parked in front of the stairs leading to the front door. Before they were out of the car, Emma appeared on the front porch to greet them.

"Mrs. Perkins, I have to say this is the most beautiful house in all of Springfield," Devan said. Linda had her hand laced through his elbow as they went up the stairs.

"Thank you for the compliment. My father built it to last. I'm sure he'd be thrilled to know it was still here." Emma held the door open for them.

Once inside, Devan and Linda were awestruck. They had walked through the foyer into the grand living room and onto the back porch before entering the gardens for the luncheon, but, they weren't in the house long enough to take in its splendor. The foyer, like the rest of the home, was beautiful. Dark wood paneling and large ceiling beams above framed a grand staircase winding to the second and third stories. A large crystal chandler hung high above illuminating the room with soft light reflecting through hundreds of decorative crystals. With the exception of a large oriental rug, two long red cushioned benches, and a large round table in the center of the room adorned with a beautiful seasonal decorative centerpiece, it was mostly empty. Yet it still radiated a sense of warmth that made the couple feel welcomed.

"Oh Devan, look. How adorable," Linda said pointing to the kitten as he made his way down the hall toward them on unsteady legs. He looked so tiny against the backdrop of the long wide hallway.

"Oh my heavens. He's loose again," Emma said. "His name is Poe and he's the newest addition to our family.

"How cute. I'm a sucker for kittens. Can I hold him?" Linda asked. Wearing a form fitting designer dress that more than flattered her shapely body, she didn't hesitate for a second to bend down to pet Poe. Devan joined her - both were smitten by the little guy. Emma got a good feeling from the couple. They didn't try to play it cool. They seemed genuine and clearly had no problem being themselves in front of others.

"Absolutely. Actually if you'd be a dear and bring him to the kitchen with me, we'll return him to his caregiver and you can meet the rest of the household." This was not Emma's original intention at all. She had planned to take the couple into the living room to entertain her guests in a more formal way. But, she changed her mind. She liked the young couple and for some reason did not feel they needed to be impressed by the grandeur of the house. At least not in the way other social elites would expect.

"Cathy, Thomas, look what we found roaming the halls," Emma said leading Devan and Linda into the kitchen as Linda affectionately held Poe close to her chest.

"Mr. Poe! Did you get out again?" Thomas asked. He was wide-eyed and surprised. He stood up, but kept his distance. Strangers made Thomas uncomfortable. His lowered eyes and hunched shoulders reflected his uneasiness.

"Linda, Devan, let me introduce you to Thomas, Poe's caregiver," Emma said. "And this is Cathy, my caregiver, live in nurse, best friend, and sometimes major pain in my rear."

Thomas wasn't the only one surprised by their sudden appearance. Cathy had been preparing the evening's dinner and wasn't expecting to be meeting the couple in the kitchen of all places. A little out of sorts, she shot Emma a stern look, but then smiled politely while trying to dry her hands..

"How embarrassing, I wasn't expecting company in the kitchen," Cathy said. "It's nice to see you, again." She shook their hands and shot Emma another look of disdain.

"Relax, Cathy. Something tells me these two don't need to be impressed by all the stuffy pretenses of a formal evening. Am I right?" Emma asked Devan and Linda.

Devan took Emma's lead. "No need to fuss over us. We're always up for free eats however we can get them," he said motioning to himself and Linda.

Linda playfully slapped his shoulder. Noticing Thomas's obvious discomfort, she addressed him directly.

"So Thomas, you're this little guys caregiver? That's great. I love kittens too. They're so cute. I think Poe is lucky to have you looking out for him. Here, I think he wants you to hold him," she said gently handing the kitten to Thomas. "How long have you had him?" she asked trying to engage Thomas.

Thomas smiled embarrassed. He was shy around strangers. "About a week. Mr. Tor brought him home."

"Who is Mr. Tor?" Linda asked. She was encouraging him and also trying to put him at ease.

"Mr. Tor is my friend. He's also a cat. He helps me around the house and yard."

"He sounds like a good friend. I hope I get to meet him tonight," she said. She smiled at Thomas.

Emma and Cathy exchanged approving looks. They liked that Linda involved him in the conversation and engaged him directly. Others usually tried to ignore Thomas, unsure of how to talk to him.

"Thomas lives in a small cottage here on the property and cares for the gardens as well as any repairs this old house may need," Emma said. She looked at him lovingly then added, "I don't know what we would do without him. He keeps this place running that's for sure."

"Thomas, I have to say, I'm impressed. We very much enjoyed walking around the gardens at the party and noticed how well kept everything is. You do a great job. The entire place is beautiful," Devan said with genuine sincerity.

Thomas stood straighter and was able to look at them. He enjoyed the attention and compliments.

"Thank you," he said with no prompting from Emma or Cathy while holding Poe and gently stroking his head.

Emma and Cathy exchanged approving looks. "Thomas, see if you can find Tor so we can introduce him to our guests, too" Emma said. Giving him a task offered an escape if he wanted to go.

"Me and Poe will find Mr. Tor and be right back," Thomas said. Smiling from ear-to-ear and with his head held high, he and Poe headed out the kitchen door on his mission.

After Thomas left, Emma filled Devan and Linda in on who Thomas was and how she came to care for him. They were moved by his story and her devotion to his care. Emma was just finishing Thomas's story, when he returned with Tor following.

"This is Mr. Tor," Thomas blurted out entering the kitchen and interrupting their conversation. Intervening quickly before anyone could address his cutting in, Devan squatted down to acknowledge Tor. He didn't immediately reach his hand out, but let Tor approach on his own. After satisfying himself that Devan was okay, Tor rubbed against Devan's knee and leg. Devan stroked him on his back.

"What a handsome guy you are. You even wore your best tux to this occasion," he said acknowledging that Tor was a tuxedo cat.

Linda, too, wasted no time greeting Tor. "You are a handsome fellow," she said scratching his head and back with her nails. Tor liked her touch and purred loudly.

Hearing the doorbell ring, Emma excused herself and returned with Jon in tow. "Entertaining in the kitchen are we?" he asked playfully joking with her.

"I'm going for a less formal approach this evening, Jon. We ordered a pizza and beer too. It should be here in a few minutes."

His look was priceless. The others laughed. "You did remember to order extra pepperonis?" Devan asked not missing a beat.

"Of course," Emma said with a sly wink and smile. Devan knew Jon well and that he was all about social etiquette. He couldn't resist picking at him a bit.

"Let's go into the living room and have cocktails while we wait for the pizza to arrive," Emma said leading the way.

"Are we really having pizza?" Thomas asked wide-eyed.

The evening passed quickly. Between the cocktails and lively conversations, all appeared to get on well. After Jon realized the others were leading him on about the pizza, he relaxed. Jon liked that Devan and Emma had so much in common despite almost fifty years separating them in age. Emma and Cathy were especially interested to hear the story of how Devan and Linda first met and then found each other again so many years later. Of course, Devan left out many juicy details leading up to their eventual reunion, but the story still told well none the less. Emma and Cathy were suckers for a good romantic tale.

Devan and Linda were fascinated with Emma's family history as well as her long career in the Navy and in nursing. She and Cathy were extraordinary women and they had the utmost respect for them both.

After dinner and more drinks, Devan and Linda finally said their goodbyes. It was late. Time had flown by as everyone entertained each other with lively stories throughout the evening. Several of the city's more colorful politicians were the subject of conversation and ridicule. Linda did excellent impersonations. She often had everyone in tears from laughing so hard. Devan also had a way of holding everyone's attention. It was obvious that both were natural entertainers and fit each other's personalities perfectly.

"Thank you for inviting us into your home and for the great dinner and conversation. I had forgotten how beautiful Springfield is. Even with much work ahead, I truly believe your goal is a worthy one. Please don't hesitate to ask me for any help you or the community might need. I'd be happy to assist where I can," Devan said. He hugged her and Cathy good night and shook Jon's hand on the front porch. Thomas had long since gone to bed.

"We were delighted to have you as our guests. To be honest, I haven't had this much fun in a long time. Thank you for coming and for your offer to help. I might just have to take you up on it," Emma said with a wink.

Emma, Cathy, and Jon waved good night to Devan and Linda as they drove down the driveway and through the gates.

"Well ladies, I think the evening went very well. Mr. Ross and his lovely wife seemed to have had a great time. Like I said before, he's a good one to have in your corner." Jon was very pleased with the outcome.

"I like Devan and Linda. It's not every day you meet people who are so comfortable being themselves. Let's keep Mr. Ross on the back burner for now. In the meantime, I need to meet with Councilman Pollock and form some kind of strategy. He is the representative for the area in question after all, so I guess he's next on our list of people to get to know better. I just hope he can stay sober long enough to help support our cause," Emma said.

Chapter
14

Sitting in his office rolling a pen between his fingers while holding the phone to his ear, Councilman Pollock was noticeably agitated.

"Yes ma'am, that's very kind of you, but I'm afraid dinner this Thursday won't be possible, I'm swamped with work." Pollock said declining Emma's dinner invitation.

"I'm sorry to hear that Mr. Pollock. Are you free for lunch one day during the week?" Emma asked.

"Oh, well... I'm not sure right now. I'll have to check my calendar and get back with you if that's ok. I'm sorry, it's just a very busy time for me right now. We have a lot of city business on the agenda at the moment." He did not want to commit.

Emma reminded him of his obligation to his constituents. "That's unfortunate. I'd very much like for us to sit down together so we can discuss how to move forward with getting those remaining blocks protected under the historical umbrella. After all, the blocks in question are in your district and many of the residents have expressed an interest in the idea."

Pollock could feel the beads of sweet forming on his forehead. He was never a good liar. "Yes ma'am. It's high on my to-do list, I can assure you of that. Since your luncheon, I've had a lot of calls about it."

"Good," Emma said. "I don't want to keep you since you're such a busy man, but I'd like to offer my assistance, home, and voice to this cause. Councilwoman Danfora has also offered to help as well. So please, check your schedule and get back with me as soon as you can. We have a lot of work ahead of us. Thank you for your time."

"Yes ma'am, I will. You have a good day now. Bye bye." When Pollock hung up he reached into his desk searching for the bottle of antacid.

Quickly shaking out three large tablets he devoured them. He sat drumming his fingers on the side of his chair.

"Why can't that old bat just mind her own business? All we needed was a few more months and this deal would have been done and over with. Now she's going to make this difficult," he said out loud to the empty room.

After a few more minutes of contemplation, Pollock took two more antacid tablets and reached for the phone. Dialing a number, he waited with uneasy anticipation for it to be picked up on the other end.

"Distinguished Councilman Pollock. Why do you honor me with this call?" The voice on the other end oozed with sarcasm.

"I'm sorry to bother you, sir, but it's about the Springfield project, it appears there might be a small problem."

"There better not be a problem Pollock. We didn't put you in that councilman's seat for you to give us problems."

"Yes sir I know, but since Emma Perkin's garden party, I've been bombarded with calls from residents wanting more information about turning those blocks into historically protected areas. And, I just hung up with Mrs. Perkins. She called to invite me to dinner or lunch to discuss moving forward with the matter. I don't know how much longer I can stall everyone."

"Just do your job, Pollock, and stop being a pussy. The deal for the warehouse complex is almost complete and soon we'll be buying up the blocks in question. Just keep the lid on for a little longer."

"I'm not sure how to do that. Perkins and Danfora are working together. I--"

"--Grow some balls Pollock! It's not Danfora's district and you need to make that clear. As to Emma Perkins, don't let some old woman fuck this up for us. Make this historical movement bullshit go away!" The phone went silent.

Pollock noticed his hands were shaking. With some effort he managed to hang up the phone before reaching for the antacid bottle. Again.

#

Emma sat at her desk in the study thinking to herself. She didn't get a good feeling from her brief conversation with Mr. Pollock, she felt like he was blowing her off.

Cathy knocked on one of the large pocket doors closing off the study from the main hall before sliding it open. "Can I come in?" she asked carrying a cup of tea for Emma.

Emma waved her in.

"You through with your call to Mr. Pollock already?" Cathy asked. She placed the cup and saucer on the desk in front of Emma.

"It was a very brief conversation," she said. She tapped her fingers on the desk lost in thought.

"Is he coming to dinner?"

"No. I even offered a lunch meeting and he said he was busy and would have to check his schedule. He said he'd get back to me as soon as he could."

"Really? What could be so important that he can't make time when summoned by Jacksonville royalty? Doesn't he know who he's dealing with?" Cathy was trying to lighten Emma's mood.

"Ha ha, Cathy. I got the impression he was trying to avoid me. I don't know why I feel like that, but I do. I'll give him a few days to get back to me, and, if I haven't heard from him by then, I'm calling back. Hell, I'll go down there if I have to!"

"That poor man has no idea who he's dealing with. Just sayin'."

"No, he doesn't," Emma said reaching for the cup of tea with cunning smile.

Chapter
15

Tuesday nights were busy for Tor. After leaving Thomas' around eight, Tor headed to the warehouse complex. The local band Tor befriended was still practicing in one of the buildings from 9:00pm to 11:00pm. For months, Tor made it a point to greet them when they arrived. He also knew Ryan would bring him a snack. He enjoyed hanging with the band prior to rehearsal and they liked him and made it a point to hang out with him. But when they rehearsed, Tor usually called it a night.

This evening started out like most. After greeting the band and eating his turkey snack offering brought by Ryan, their lead singer, Tor retreated to the alley next to the building to satisfy his other nightly cravings. Being the seasoned hunter that he was, it wasn't long before he'd killed two large rats. That was usually his limit.

Rats and mice were his typical prey. After killing them, he'd often play with the lifeless bodies, knocking them around and running after them. When tiring of his morbid game, he'd leave the bodies outside the warehouse door prompting several of the band members to nickname him "Killer". The band respected his hunting skills and looked forward to seeing what the body count was when they wrapped later in the evening. Having already made his kills for the night and leaving them prominently displayed outside the warehouse doors, Tor relaxed on an elevated pile of wooden pallets bathing himself and occasionally looking through the window next to him where he could see the band members performing.

Hearing the sound of barking dogs rapidly approaching, he crouched down on top of the pallets to conceal himself. Suddenly, a small brown cat ran into the alley desperately looking for a place to hide. In a panic, it darted under the pile of pallets beneath Tor. A large dog came racing into the alley barking and growling in hot pursuit. The small brown cat was trapped. The dog had him pinned under the crates and was viciously attacking through the openings.

Tor's eyes ignited in a blinding rage. He leapt from the top of the crate, onto the attacking dog sinking his claws and teeth into its back and neck. Howling, the dog collapsed writhing in excruciating pain. Tor was draining its energy, its life force, with amazing efficiency. The dog cried out again, but was becoming more helpless with every passing second as Tor hung on.

Unseen by Tor, another dog ran into the alley. Not hesitating, the second dog viciously attacked Tor, ripping him from the first dog's back and violently shaking him in his mouth ripping a large gash in his back leg. Fighting back, Tor scratched the dog's head with his razor-sharp claws ripping off a large piece of its right ear causing the dog to release its grip and throw Tor hard across the alley. In the chaos and confusion, the small brown cat ran out from under the pallets and escaped into the darkness before two more dogs entered the alley barking excitedly. The three dogs had Tor pinned in a corner and the fourth was recovering quickly. Badly injured, Tor could not leap to the safety of the elevated pallets and was forced to stand his ground. Trapped, there was no escape.

# # #

"Sounds great everyone. Take five and when we come back lets run through the new songs one more time then call it a night," Allen said, speaking to his fellow band members. The warehouse was hot. Even though it was later in the evening, the humid night air created a stuffy atmosphere inside the building.

"Ok, gentlemen, but after that I have to go. I have a 9:00am meeting," Ryan said half joking half serious as he placed the microphone back in its stand. Having been singing almost nonstop for an hour, he welcomed the short break.

"No worries, buddy. We know you're head honcho in that advertising firm of yours. You'll have plenty of time to get home and get your beauty sleep," Allen said.

Ryan shot Allen a bird. "I'll be outside getting some fresh air," he laughed shaking his head. He grabbed a towel off a nearby table to wipe the sweat from his face as he walked toward the large open warehouse door.

"When are you going to quit that corporate rat race? It's going to make you old before your time!"

Truth be known, the band respected Ryan's decision to keep his full time job. They knew they were lucky to get what time they could with him. After losing their original lead singer, the band stumbled across Ryan in a bar one evening and the rest was history. Ryan was the youngest partner and by all accounts, the most successful, in a rapidly expanding regional advertising agency. He loved his work and made it known early on that that was his main priority. Having joined the band a year earlier at their request to help record material they were trying to market, Ryan stayed on and soon helped propel them to the top of the local music scene. He enjoyed singing and on occasion found ways to combine both professions. He was amazingly talented in many arenas, yet, had the maturity and discipline to stay focused on his objectives.

Walking out of the warehouse to retrieve his phone from the car, he heard a loud commotion coming from the alley. Hearing dogs barking, he immediately thought of Tor and ran over to investigate. To his horror, his fears were confirmed. A pack of wild dogs had Tor backed into a corner and were attacking him. Ryan grabbed a piece of lumber from a scrap pile and ran at the dogs but they didn't retreat. Instead, they turned their attention to Ryan and lunged for him. But this was a big mistake. Ryan swung the board hard slamming it into the side of two of the more aggressive dogs' heads and bodies knocking them across the alley. He managed to get between the other dogs and Tor taking up a defensive position holding them off. Recovered, the other two dogs advanced growling and barking. Ryan stepped forward swinging wildly knocking them back again. This last impact must have hurt because they whimpered and ran to a safer distance. Ryan charged after them yelling and swinging the piece of wood wildly like a crazy man. Having had enough, the pack turned tail and ran out of the alley.

Returning to Tor, Ryan saw he was pretty beat up. He was wet and covered in saliva and blood. Tor tried to get up, but was too unsteady and couldn't stand. There was a large gash on his left back leg. Scared, Tor tried to get up again, but his leg did not cooperate. In an attempt to calm him, Ryan sat on the ground and pat his head and back lightly, Tor settled down but was clearly rattled. Seeing the cat injured touched Ryan deeply. Realizing he needed serious medical attention, Ryan looked at his tag again, but saw no phone number only an address. Realizing it was close by, Ryan wrapped Tor in the towel he'd taken from the warehouse and took him to his car. He was going to try to find the address, but if he couldn't, he would take him to a 24-hour emergency clinic close to his house.

"Sorry guys. I have to cut it short tonight," Ryan said to his confused band member friends as he drove out of the parking lot with Tor in his lap.

As Tor sat curled up under the towel, his eyes began to glow lightly. Ryan felt what he thought was a sudden increase in Tor's body heat radiating through the towel. "Wow, bud. You really run hot." He drove feeling the uncomfortable heat. But given what Tor had just been through, Ryan sucked it up and dealt with the discomfort.

Unknown to Ryan, the heat he was feeling wasn't just Tor's body heat. The cut on his leg was also glowing with the same intensity as his eyes. Because he was covered up under the towel, Ryan couldn't see his eyes or leg glowing as the cut slowly began to heal.

Finally becoming unbearable, Ryan shifted in his seat and slightly adjusted Tor on his lap. Feeling the heat instantly dissipate when he shifted position, Ryan said out loud, "Ah, that's better."

Minutes later Ryan pulled up to a large gate. The address embossed in large steel numbers across the top corresponded to the one on the tag. Needless to say, he was surprised such an impressive home was located in this area. Wasting no time he walked to the gate and pushed a buzzer intercom. Within seconds a voice responded. "Yes? Can I help you?"

"Hi. My name is Ryan Anderson. I apologize for bothering you so late, but I think I have your cat with me. He was in a fight with some dogs and appears pretty badly injured. I saw the address on the tag so I brought him here. I don't mean to be rude, but if money is an issue I'll be happy to take him to an emergency vet clinic and cover any expenses."

There was a slight pause. "Thank you but that won't be necessary. Please wait there, I'll be right out."

Ryan cradled Tor in his arms as he leaned against his car. Cathy made her way to the front gate quickly. When she saw Ryan holding Tor her face showed both relief and concern. Ryan didn't look like the thugs that typically roamed the neighborhood streets after dark, and seeing Tor being held so caringly in the young man's arms alleviated any concerns she had about the stranger on the other side of the gate.

"What happened to him?" she asked. Her voice gave away her emotion.

"He was in a fight. Some dogs were getting the better of him when I showed up. I broke up the fight, but it looks like the poor guy got it pretty good. I wanted to get him home, but I'm serious about getting him care if you would like me to – no charge. I like this guy. He's always hanging around the warehouse a few blocks from here where my band and I rehearse. We've kinda bonded." Ryan tried to mask his growing concern for Tor.

"I appreciate that, but I'm a nurse as is the woman who owns this house. If we can't help him then nobody can." Reaching for the cat, Ryan handed him to her. Tor looked at Ryan and softly whimpered. It was sad and Ryan was choked up. "You get better buddy. Hope to see you at our next rehearsal."

Taking Tor, Cathy looked at him. "It's ok young fellow, you're in good hands." She turned to Ryan. "Thank you for bringing him home. I'm Cathy Barton. I'm a live-in nurse and caregiver for Emma Perkins. Tor is her baby. Seeing him like this is going to break her heart," she said.

"Again, I'm really sorry. Here, please take my card and if there's anything you need to help him get better don't hesitate to ask." Ryan tucked his business card in the towel with Tor.

"Thank you. That's very kind." Turning to go back inside the compound, Cathy stopped and looked back to Ryan. "Tor's lucky to have you as his friend." She shut the gate and carried Tor back to the house.

Ryan was relieved, but still had his concerns. When he got back to his car he felt exhausted, like his energy level had taken a big hit. He sat there for a few minutes trying to shake the feeling. Knowing his band mates were probably wondering what happened to him, he finally cranked up the car and headed back to the warehouse still feeling out of sorts.

# # #

Emma was half way down the main staircase when Cathy came through the front door carrying Tor in the towel. She was usually not one to startle easy, but when she saw the blood soaked towel, her heart sank. "How bad is it?" Emma asked in a broken tone.

"I'm not sure yet. The young man who brought him home said he'd been attacked by some dogs. Let's get him to the kitchen so we can see what we're dealing with," Cathy said. She pushed back her personal feelings and let the professional nurse inside take over.

Like Cathy, Emma knew this was not the time to get emotional. As if a switch flipped, she took a deep breath then set about gathering everything she thought they would need to treat Tor's injuries.

Cathy carried Tor to the kitchen where the light was better and placed him on the kitchen table. Still wrapped in the towel, Tor remained calm. Cathy and Emma prepared a clean makeshift trauma center on one of the kitchen counters preparing for all eventualities. When they were ready, Cathy placed Tor on the sterilized counter. Carefully unwrapping the bloody towel, they dreaded what they would find. When Cathy pulled back the last layer of towel they were startled by what they saw. Or didn't see. Though covered from head to toe in blood, they could find no visible sign of a major injury. Other than a small cut on one of his back legs, he seemed ok. Satisfied he had no serious external injuries, Cathy carefully bathed him in the sink. Surprisingly compliant, Tor remained calm as Cathy cleaned the blood and grime from his coat. When she finished, she dried him with a towel.

"You were lucky, boy," Cathy said, rubbing him down. Tor stood calmly on the counter as Cathy dried him off and again looked him over for other injuries.

"Where did the young man say he found him?" Emma asked.

"Over in the warehouse complex. He said Tor hangs out with them when he and his band rehearse. I guess he's some kind of musician."

Shaking her head, Emma reached over and gently stroked Tor's back. "My, what an interesting life you live, boy." Briefly, she thought maybe it would be best to keep him inside, but then thought better. Who was she to lock him up? Tor was a free spirit and she knew keeping him locked away from the outside world would eventually be a death sentence. Taking a deep breath, more out of relief, Emma said, "It's a dangerous world out there my friend, please be careful. I don't know what I would do if anything happened to you."

Tor started purring loudly and perked up. He walked to the edge of the counter and affectionately nudged Emma with his head acting like his old self. "Yeah. I love you, too." She returned his affection with a gentle hug.

Satisfied he was clean and had no major injuries, Cathy and Emma applied some antiseptic to the small cut on his leg.

"I wonder where all this blood came from?" Cathy asked. She placed the towel on the kitchen table. "The young man who brought him here was so concerned. He said Tor had taken a pretty good working over. Looking at him now all cleaned up, he seems ok to me."

"Maybe the blood wasn't all his? Knowing this slick rascal, I bet he got a few good licks in himself," Emma said.

"You're probably right. Something tells me Tor knows how to look out for himself."

For being such a good patient Emma spread a little whip cream in a bowl and gave it to him on the counter. "Here buddy, your favorite. I think you've earned it tonight," she said as they watched him lap up the cream.

Seeing a business card lying next to the towel Emma picked it up and read it. "Ryan Anderson. It says he's in advertising. Huh, good to know," she said, placing the card in her pocket.

Chapter
16

A few weeks later, Emma tried to call Councilman Pollock, but was repeatedly told he was not available. After several more attempts by phone, she and Cathy decided to pay Pollock a visit at city hall in person.

"What do you mean he's not available? We were told downstairs that he was here and in his office. You're telling me he's not here. Where is he then?" Cathy insisted as she spoke to Pollock's assistant.

"I'm sorry, but you just missed him. He's in a meeting with the port authority for the rest of the day. If you would like to make an appointment, I'd be happy to set something up." Pollock's assistant was flustered at this point. It was obvious she was trying to cover for her boss and didn't like doing it.

"When's the next available appointment?" Cathy asked.

Nervously thumbing through the appointment book she tried to hide a note she wrote to herself to not schedule any appointments with Emma Perkins or pass on her phone calls until further notice. Knowing she was going to have to do something in order to resolve the situation and get Cathy and Emma to leave, she offered them an appointment for the following afternoon at two o'clock.

"We'll be here. Tell Mr. Pollock he'd better be here this time," Emma said not attempting to hide her irritation.

After they left, Pollock peered around his office door. "Are they gone?" he asked.

"They're gone for now. But to get them to leave, I had to schedule an appointment for tomorrow at 2 o'clock." His assistant was irritated.

"What? Why did you do that? I can't see them tomorrow."

"They wouldn't have left if I didn't offered something to calm them down." Her voice was getting high

"Ok, ok. I get it. Tomorrow at 11o'clock, call her and tell her I've been detained and will have to reschedule for next week."

"Why? You're here tomorrow."

Now Pollock was really irritated. "Just do your job or I'll find someone who can."

He went back into his office and shut the door a little too hard.

"Prick!" she said under her breath.

# # #

After receiving the cancellation call from Pollock's assistant, Emma was livid. She called Councilwoman Danfora for help.

"He's been avoiding you for weeks?" she asked surprised.

"Yes. I've tried to get a hold of him numerous times and every time he's either busy or not available. I'm really sorry to bother you with this. What do you suggest?" Emma asked.

"Let me have a crack at him. I'll go over to his office myself and try to find out what's going on. I'll call you back in a little while."

"Thank you so much. I know these blocks are not your responsibility but I do appreciate all your help," Emma said with genuine admiration.

"We'll get to the bottom of this. I can assure you of that," the Councilwoman said before hanging up.

Emma sat dumbfounded wondering what was going on. Why was Pollock avoiding her? She is not in his district but still, she's offering to help spread awareness and organize the residents for nothing. All she wants to do is restore her little part of Jacksonville to make the area great again. She couldn't understand why he was so unwilling to help? She realized there was nothing more she could do for now but wait.

# # #

Councilwoman Sonya Danfora was a petite, attractive woman and formidable when she had to be. Walking up to Pollock's assistant she simply asked, "Is he in?"

"Yes," she answered with a friendly smile.

The Councilwoman smiled and walked by her.

"Wait! I'll announce you," his assistance screeched nearly in a panic.

She ignored her and continued right into his office shutting the door behind her.

Caught off guard, Pollock looked surprised as he stood up from behind his desk. "Councilwoman Danfora, what can I do for you?"

"Emma Perkins said she's been trying to get a hold of you, but you won't return her calls. Is there a problem?"

He was pissed. How dare she confront him? "No! There's not a problem. I'll get back to Mrs. Perkins just as soon as I can."

"She thinks your purposely avoiding her. Are you sure there's not a problem?"

"Let me remind you Mrs. Perkins does not reside in my district. Her needs do not take precedent over those of the people I represent. I'll get back to Mrs. Perkins just as soon as time allows," he said. He was still pissed at her nerve.

"All she wants is to talk with you about helping the people you represent obtain a historical designation. I would think you'd be on board with that. Just look what it's done for my district."

"I know what she wants! As to what's best for my constituents, I think I'm better qualified to make that determination than you. It is my district we're talking about."

"Yes, but--"

"--that will be enough. I have not asked for your help nor do I want it! Besides, the citizens occupying the blocks in question haven't shown interest in pursuing it and until they do, I won't be wasting my time on this issue. Now, I'd appreciate it if you'd leave my office."

Even though Pollock expressed great conviction when speaking to the councilwoman, she could tell he was clearly uncomfortable. Noticing him shaking and sweating profusely, she decided to drop her interrogation - for now anyway. Truth be told, she was a little worried he was going to have a heart attack or a stroke.

"Have it your way. But I can guarantee one thing, you haven't heard the last from us. Not by a long shot." she said giving him an "eat shit" look before walking out.

A few minutes later she was on the phone with Emma telling her about their encounter.

"What does he mean the residents aren't interested? Many are interested. We've been talking to people daily since the party. You've been kind enough to take calls from all those who had questions about the process and what it means to have a historical designation," Emma said. She was becoming more aggravated by the minute.

"That's why I don't believe him either," Sonya said. "But for now, sit tight and let me do more investigating on my end. I'll see if I can figure out what's really going on."

Still not happy, Emma reluctantly agreed and thanked the councilwoman again for all her help. After hanging up, Emma sat at her desk contemplating the situation. She didn't like Pollock. From their first meeting, she had a bad feeling about him. Then she remembered the interaction between him and Devan at the party. Remembering what Jon said about Devan and how his mere presence is enough to make some city officials and other social elites uncomfortable, she began to devise a plan. "Mr. Ross, I hope your offer to help still stands," she said out loud.

Chapter
17

"It's so nice to see you again, Devan," Emma said greeting Devan warmly on the front porch of her house as he walked up the stairs.

She smiled and took his arm leading him into the house. "I'm so pleased you accepted my invitation to lunch."

"I was looking forward to seeing you again. Linda and I were planning to have you and your group over one evening for dinner once we get settled into our new place."

"We look forward to your invitation," she said, leading him through the living room and out into a large octagonal glass and steel framed atrium attached to the rear of the house by a beautiful set of leaded glass French doors. A fan was slowly spinning high above creating a gentle breeze - not that it was needed. The weather could not have been more perfect. Beautiful, well cared for plants surrounded a cobblestone patio with a simple white iron table and chairs in the center.

Devan saw that the table was prepared for two. "Are Cathy and Thomas joining us?" he asked.

"Not this time. I have to admit, I invited you here to discuss a little problem I have. And I hear through the grapevine that you have some influence in such matters," she said and motioned for him to take a seat.

"I'm intrigued." Devan settled into his chair.

Emma was not one to mince words. Taking the seat across from him, she got right to the point.

"At my party I noticed the interaction between you and Councilman Pollock. To be frank, he appeared down right terrified of you. And to be completely honest, I have to admit, I enjoyed watching that little weasel squirm," she said.

Devan could see she was enjoying this, but his expression was blank. He figured she had checked into him and given who she was in the community, assumed she had access to credible sources. The question on Devan's mind was, how much did she know. Not one to give away his hand, he remained silent. This meeting was at her request, so he let her put her cards on the table.

Emma studied him trying to gauge a reaction. Was he an ally or the enemy? She still wasn't sure. She got a good first impression from him at her party, as well as when he came for dinner, but now, sitting across from her, she could tell he had another side, one she had not yet met. So she pushed farther.

"And after talking with others, it appears you seem to have that effect on many of our city's elite – both social and elected. I have to say Devan, that's a pretty impressive talent. May I ask how you came to acquire it?"

He looked her directly in the eye and held his gaze. It was almost long enough to make her feel uncomfortable. He softened his expression. "Let's just say I was in the right place at the right time to acquire a lot of personal information about certain individuals."

Emma was pleased. She wasn't sure how he would respond to her comment if he responded at all, but he did. He could have denied everything, played ignorant, or even become offended and left. Instead, he indicated he was willing to dance with her - at least for now.

Cathy checked on them and asked if they cared for a cocktail before lunch was served. "How about a drink Devan? I know I could use one," Emma said.

Devan didn't know where Emma was going with any of this, but he had to respect her style. Emma had class. It had been sometime since anyone had the balls to approach him as directly as she had. He nodded in agreement. "Jim Beam on the rocks would be nice."

"Make that two please, Cathy." Cathy nodded and left the atrium to prepare the drinks. She was not offended by Emma's dismissal. She knew Emma was on a mission. She'd seen it many times before.

"My father use to say you can tell a lot about a man from the kind of liquor he drank," Emma said.

"Is that so? What does whiskey say about me?" he asked curious of her response.

"You prefer the dark liquors which indicates you're confident, you order what you want. You have no need or desire to impress others with pretentious posturing. You are who you are and make no effort to be anything else." She smiled and then added, "Like me."

Cathy brought their drinks then left the room.

Devan raised his glass and said, "Here's to the whiskey drinkers of the world."

Emma raised her glass and clinked his.

They both took a healthy swig. "So, tell me about this problem you have," Devan said.

Over lunch, Emma explained her frustration with Councilman Pollock. She told Devan that since her garden party she and Cathy - along with the help of Councilwoman Danfora - had been busy organizing the residents and business owners associated with the blocks in question. She told him there was an almost unanimous interest in proceeding with historical designation. Unable to reach Mr. Pollock themselves, many had reached out to Emma and Councilwoman Danfora for information. Emma told Devan how she'd been trying for weeks to contact Pollock in an effort to help create some kind of plan but he appeared to be avoiding her on purpose. She also shared what Councilwoman Danfora said happened when she went to see him in his office. After her confrontation with Pollock, Emma was completely baffled. She couldn't understand why he was being so uncooperative. Feeling like she had run out of options she turned to Devan for help.

When she finished, Emma sat back in her chair and crossed her arms frustrated. The gesture reminded him of a frustrated kid denied of some much wanted candy. He couldn't help but smile.

"I agree. It sounds like he's avoiding you. More to the point, it sounds like he's not interested in helping protect those blocks. So the question is, why?"

"That's the most frustrating part. The majority of the people he claims to represent want this. It'll benefit the area. I would think he'd be bending over backwards to help. Instead, it seems he's going out of his way to avoid dealing with his own constituents. What's up with that?" she asked.

"I don't know, but I'm intrigued. Maybe our honorable Councilman answers to someone else," Devan proposed.

Emma's eyebrows rose as she suddenly remembered something. "That prick!"

"Excuse me?" Devan asked, amused.

"The mayor! His father's company bought the warehouse complex bordering those blocks last year, also in Pollock's district. I'd completely forgotten about that. Do you think they're pulling his strings?" she asked.

"Could be. His Honor's father has made a fortune in real estate by screwing over others for decades, often at the expense of the little guy. Maybe they have other plans for those blocks," Devan suggested. Emma sat bolt upright in her chair.

"It'll be a cold day in hell before I let that little weasel twerp or his lousy father tear down one more house on any of those blocks," Emma said. Devan was amused by her resolved.

"Give me a few days to look into this," Devan said as he gestured with his hands for her to calm down. "If the mayor or anyone in his family are behind Pollock's unwillingness to cooperate, this could prove to be very enlightening on many fronts. In the meantime, I suggest you step up your efforts in uniting the residents behind your cause. If you can rally enough people, it'll be impossible for him to ignore." Pausing for a second he had an idea. "I know a few people in the press who might be interested in your story. Actually, I'm sure they'll be interested in your story. I'll have them give you a call tomorrow. The sooner you get some public visibility the better. It's been my experience that people who like doing business in the dark usually back away when a bright light is shined in their direction," he said.

"That would be wonderful! Thank you," Emma replied. "I'll do what I can, Devan, but I still need more help. I was counting on Pollock, but I guess that's not going to happen. And poor councilwoman Danfora. She's been so helpful, but those blocks are not in her district. I feel bad for asking so much of her."

"I'll loan you my assistant, Cindy Clark. I think you two will get along great. She's not one to take 'no' for an answer, either. In the meantime, let me dig into this and see what turns up." They had finished lunch and he stood up to leave.

"Thank you, Devan. I really appreciate your help. Pollock is up to something. I can feel it."

"Don't fret over it too much. I know how to deal with politicians like our good Mr. Pollock."

"Just for the record, I've dealt with my share of bureaucrats over the years too," she said. Devan nodded reading between the lines. "Until our next meeting then. Good afternoon Mrs. Perkins."

"Good afternoon Mr. Ross."

As Emma watched Devan drive down the driveway she couldn't help but smile. *Maybe having him in my corner is a good thing after all.*

Chapter
18

On the drive back to his office, Devan called his most trusted associate and number two man, Jamison West. At 6'4" with a solid muscular physique to match, Jamison's mere presence had an intimidating effect on those around him, something Devan frequently used to his advantage. Having been discharged from the Navy Seals after a serious injury on a classified mission, Jamison had a hard time coping with life out of the service, which resulted in several brushes with the law that ultimately limited his employment options. Devan met Jamison on one of his construction crews and they developed an immediate friendship. His military background and ability to lead others got Devan's attention. After his two primary business partners suddenly decided to retire, he looked within his organization for someone he could trust to fill their void. Jamison stood out and the rest was history. Not only did Devan rely on him professionally, but also personally. Next to his wife, Jamison is the only other person he truly trusts. He called Jamison on the way back to his office

"I need you to check into something for me," Devan said.

"Sure, Boss. What's up?"

"Looks like Big Daddy Douglas and the mayor are planning something in Springfield with that old warehouse complex. Can you see what you can dig up? Also see what connection Councilman Pollock has to Douglas. I think Douglas has him on a short leash and I need to know why."

"I'm on it."

Devan knew the current mayor had his job only because his father, John Douglas Sr. bought it for him. He was known as "Big Daddy" to Devan and Jamison; "JD" to his friends. Devan never pretended to be his friend nor did he have any respect for the man or his family. The Douglas' used their wealth and influence to dominate Jacksonville politics for years often at the expense of others. That is until Devan was forced to fight back after being double-crossed by the city's power elite in a business deal many years ago.

Through a fortunate and orchestrated sequence of events, Devan and his business partners at the time obtained a vast amount of embarrassing and potentially disastrous personal information involving many of the city's movers and shakers. Knowing there was more to be gained by having such information and not using it, Devan turned the tables on his double-crossers as well as a corrupt network overflowing with the privileged power-elite creating a comfortable position for himself. Behind the scenes and out of the public eye, Devan wielded the real power and had no problem reminding others of that fact. Occasionally, a more physical confrontation might be called for and here, Jamison proved handy.

It was never Devan's intent to permanently remain "in charge" of Jacksonville's many corrupt power brokers. Originally, he only wanted what was denied to him and his associates after he was double-crossed. But, as time passed, he found himself transitioning into more of a "Godfather" role – the gangster version, of course. Even the powerful elite need some form of structure – rules to play by. As his position evolved, Devan found himself resolving disputes between different factions/families/organizations, etc., in an effort to keep the peace. The city's uncontrolled growth proved destructive, requiring a strong hand to bring a form of balance and justice beyond the rule of law. He knew this was a screwed up system, but when looking at who the other major players were, he felt he was the most morally and ethically qualified to head it up. Who else could be trusted? He learned early on there was nothing money couldn't buy and political power and influence were for sale across the city. So for now, he was content. He told himself someone had to look out for the little guy and figured that someone might as well be him. And, of course, there was something to be said about lording over so many arrogant assholes.

On the drive back to his office he thought about all the corruption and quasi-legal closed door secret business deals he constantly found himself confronted with. The real movers and shakers of the community were not in the public eye. They existed in the background, unseen by anyone, choosing to do their bidding through those they influenced and controlled by various means. Despite his best efforts to exert some manor of control over these activities, the task was daunting. "The American Way," he said out loud to himself.

# # #

Cathy and Tor met Emma in the foyer after she returned from walking Devan out.

"So? How did everything go with the dreamy Mr. Ross?" Cathy asked swooning and pretending to fan herself.

Emma smiled and took Cathy by the arm. "I have a feeling we'll be hearing from Councilman Pollock very soon," she said. She walked with Cathy to the kitchen so they could start preparing the evening's dinner. Tor was meowing excitedly knowing they would spoil him as they cooked.

Chapter
19

Devan was about to call it a night when Jamison walked into his office.

"I have that information you wanted."

"That was fast. I figured you'd need at least a day," Devan joked.

"It wasn't hard to find. The entire warehouse complex was bought by Big Daddy Douglas's company last year. Rumor has it they plan to demolish the complex and build quite the residential community. Townhomes, high-rise buildings, businesses, the works. Looks like it could be a real boon for the area."

"Ok, so far so good. What's with Pollock? Why is he refusing to help Mrs. Perkins and the other residents with their historical agenda and how does he fit in to all this?"

Jamison sat down across from Devan. "This is where things get interesting. It appears our honorable councilman use to work for Big Daddy. He decided to run for office one day and with heavy financial support from Big Daddy himself. He won."

"Doesn't explain why he refuses to help Emma and the other residents."

"Actually, it does. From what I've gathered through the grapevine, those eight blocks are to be part of the new development."

"Bingo!" Devan said. "Big Daddy can't demolish them if they're protected. Now it makes sense why Pollock is dodging his constituents and Emma. He's been given orders to not let this happen."

"So what's your angle? Are you interested in getting a piece of the action?" Jamison asked.

Devan smiled his usual devil-may-care-smile. "All in good time. For now, I promised Mrs. Perkins I'd look into why Pollock has been dodging her. Now I know. Thanks, man. "

"All in a day's work," Jamison said as he got up to leave. "If there's nothing else, I'm calling it a night."

"I'm not too far behind you. Have a good evening."

After Jamison left Devan picked up the phone and made his call.

# # #

While tidying up her desk in preparation to go home for the evening, Julie Armstrong, personal assistant to Mr. John Douglas Sr., CEO of Douglas Investments and Real Estate Inc., answered the ringing phone.

"Yes sir. He's still here. Please hold." Julie trotted down the hall and into a small conference room.

"Mr. Douglas you have a call from Devan Ross. He says it's important."

Looking at a business associate sitting across from him, John's expression immediately showed his concern.

"I wonder what he wants?" the man asked.

"I don't know," John said reaching for the phone. "Mr. Ross, this is an unexpected surprise, what can I do for you?"

"Good evening, JD. I was hoping you could help me with a small problem. Do you think you can find time this evening to discuss it in person?"

John Douglas Sr., the patriarch of one of the richest old money families in Jacksonville, head of his family's thriving real estate development company as well as dozens of other successful business enterprises, was not a man who just dropped everything. Pausing before responding to Devan, a million things ran through his head.

"Perhaps my timing is bad," Devan said noticing the long pause.

"Sorry, I was just looking at my schedule. I can swing by your office if you're still there on my way home. Thirty minutes?"

"See you in thirty," Devan said.

"What was that about?" his associate asked.

"I have no idea." Genuine concern registered on his face.

# # #

Even though their financial interests spread far and wide, the bulk of the Douglas family wealth came from real estate. They owned thousands of acres throughout the county. Many of the more popular residential and retail shopping centers were Douglas developments. As Jacksonville grew, their power and influence also expanded. By the early 2000's, they were easily one of the most powerful families in the city and they let people know it. Through intimidation, bribes, pay-offs, and other means, they controlled or manipulated many officials across the county and city. There was nothing their money couldn't buy.

As Jacksonville continued to prove popular to individuals and companies looking to relocate, JD, along with other wealthy and influential members of the community realized that as all this new wealth poured into Jacksonville, they faced the possibility that their influence and power might one day be diluted and even replaced by others. Deciding it was imperative they stay in charge, they formed an underground, secret city government consisting of the "real" movers and shakers of the community. For decades they owned the city, bending it to their will. That is, until one of the group's members decided to double-cross Devan and his partners.

Like many in Jacksonville, Devan's family had also been burned by this corruption. Having heard the stories about what happened to his grandfather when he tangled with the establishment, Devan knew how the system worked. He knew there was a way of doing things and how the game was supposed to be played. But, when he was confronted with an incident involving a real estate project of his own, he fought back and not in the conventional sense. Oh no. Devan and his partners took it to a whole new level - one the establishment never saw coming.

Since he knew he could never fight them in the courts - they owned them, too - he settled for another way. Blackmail.

Over a short period of time Devan and his accomplices accumulated an enormous amount of embarrassing information on most the city's key figures. Even if they couldn't get a specific individual, they caught someone close enough to that person to still prove useful. After they gathered their ammunition, Devan arranged a meeting with the most senior members of this exclusive group. There, he let them know exactly what he had. Through photos, audio, video, and an endless stream of physical documentation linking them and many others to all kinds of illegal, immoral, and fraudulent activities, Devan threatened to expose them all. The threat alone was enough to change the balance of power. By the end of that meeting, Devan was firmly in control.

The arrogance and belief that those privileged elite were free to do whatever they wanted to whomever they wanted whenever they wanted with no fear of the consequences gave them a false feeling of security. They believed they were above the law and untouchable in their little Jacksonville kingdom. And "Big Daddy Douglas" was one of the worst. It turned out John Douglas Sr. had a strong lust for young sexual partners –women and men. He insisted they call him "Big Daddy", thus Devan and Jamison's nickname for him. The man so disgusted Devan that he and Jamison often contemplated beating the shit out of him just for the hell of it. But, knowing that would compromise their position, Devan chose to deal with him another way. After sharing some extremely embarrassing video with John Douglas Sr. in a specially arranged closed door meeting at Devan's office, "Big Daddy" suddenly had new respect for Devan.

Chapter 20

Devan owned two of the most popular entertainment venues in Jacksonville. One was a downtown hot spot called The Excalibur. This was a multi-thousand square foot building converted into several levels of entertainment space. Local bands preformed there on weekends to crowds of thousands. From the time the doors opened, it proved to be a success for people of all ages and backgrounds.

The other, was the popular San Marco night club, The Vault. Occupying an entire block of trendy historic San Marco, was an old bank building that Devan had converted into a popular upscale club and multi-level restaurant. A large section of the second floor had also been converted into his company headquarters. Here, he oversaw all aspects of his thriving local empire. For many, this was the real seat of Jacksonville's power.

John Douglas Sr. wasted no time getting to Devan's office. Entering through the back entrance, an armed security guard accompanied him to a private elevator and escorted him to Devan's office. Devan took his security seriously. $10 an hour security guards would not do. He only employed the best trained ex-military men and women for all his security needs. Paying well above average, he made sure the company headquarters was guarded 24/7 by only the most competent. This typically un-nerved visitors giving Devan an advantage in negotiations. Those "summoned to appear before him" tended to be overtly respectful and agreeable when surrounded by the tense military-like atmosphere.

"JD. It's nice to see you again," Devan said standing up behind his desk as John was escorted into his office.

Shaking hands, Devan nodded to the guard and he left the room closing the door behind him.

Hearing the door close made small beads of perspiration appear on JD's head. Devan observed his nervousness and offered him a seat across from his desk.

"I have to say I wasn't expecting to hear from you. How can I help you?" JD asked. He fidgeted in his chair.

Devan looked at him with cold, empty eyes holding him in his gaze long enough to make him feel even more uncomfortable before responding. "It appears we have a common interest in Springfield."

Pretending to be surprised JD tried to regain his composure. "Really? What interest is that?" he asked already knowing the answer.

"The old warehouse complex you bought last year. I hear you have big plans for that place and the surrounding area."

"Oh, that, yes, well...yes...we're looking at developing some of that in the next few years," he replied. He was obviously trying to downplay the extent of the project.

Devan simply smiled. "From what I hear it's a pretty significant commitment. Commercial, residential, high rise buildings, the works. Looks pretty substantial to me."

"Well, yes, over the next few years we plan to bring it on in phases. Speaking of which, I was planning to approach you about using your construction company. I was hoping we could come to some kind of arrangement." JD thought this was why he had been summoned.

"That's awfully kind of you, JD, but that's not why I asked you hear."

JD was perplexed, but showed no emotion.

"You see, I'm more interested in those eight blocks outside the complex. You know the ones trying to get a historical designation. Actually, a good friend of mine, you may know her, Emma Carson Perkins, and a group of residents have been organizing to have their area covered by the historical umbrella so their properties are protected. My friend asked me to find out why their elected representative, Councilman Pollock, is refusing to assist them in their worthy cause. Surely your large project doesn't include razing those blocks? I mean destroying some of Jacksonville's earliest historically significant residences would be a serious loss for the entire community."

JD knew he was caught. Devan knew exactly what he intended to do with those blocks. Realizing that Devan was telling him this was not a good idea, he choose his next words more out of frustration than angst.

"I had no idea you'd taken such an interest in preserving our city's past."

"Mrs. Perkins opened my eyes to the forgotten beauty of Springfield," Devan said looking at him with a disapproving look acknowledging his frustrated response.

At this point, JD was trembling with both fear and anger. "Of course those blocks can be spared. Actually, they'd add character to our project. That's a great idea," he added with forced enthusiasm.

Even though Devan had gotten what he wanted and was enjoying turning the screws in the asshole before him, he had a reputation for being fair, so he threw JD a bone. "That's good news. And FYI, I know the Port Authority wants to unload a sizable section of property bordering the south side of the warehouse complex. If memory serves me, it even includes some nice waterfront access. I'm sure they'd offer you a fair price," Devan said. Devan was giving JD an even better deal than the eight blocks. Truth be known, Devan had been offered the Port Authority property and was holding an option to buy it. Letting JD purchase it instead and then partnering to do the primary construction work was actually more lucrative for Devan. This way he didn't have to spend any of his money, but would still benefit by being part of the project.

JD's face beamed with both relief and excitement. He realized this would allow him to take his project to a whole new level. Unable to contain his excitement he jumped up from his chair.

"That's a great idea! I'll get with the project planners first thing in the morning so we can start redesigning the layout. Waterfront access is a major game changer!" he said. "And then, as soon as we have a new plan, I'll call you so we can work out the specifics of your end." JD's excitement was genuine. He felt like he'd made a deal with the devil and lived to tell about it.

"That's great, JD. I'm glad we could come to an understanding. I look forward working with you on this project. As to the eight blocks, I assume the honorable Councilman Pollock will have a sudden change of heart and help Mrs. Perkins and the other residents in their quest to gain their historical protection?"

"I can assure you he will be most cooperative," JD said and extended his hand to Devan.

"I can't wait to tell Mrs. Perkins," Devan said shaking his hand. Unseen by JD, Devan had pushed a button summoning a security guard to his office. Within seconds there was a knock on his door and the guard entered. "Please escort Mr. Douglas out."

"Yes sir." The security guard looked at JD with ice cold military eyes. Catching the meaning, JD hastily said goodbye.

"What a douche bag," Devan uttered under his breath before returning to his desk. He picked up his phone to make a call.

Chapter
21

After dinner, Emma, Cathy, and Thomas sat around the kitchen table recapping the day's events. Thomas was particularly talkative. He'd made great progress with the new plantings Emma requested. Given her on-going role in helping drive the historical campaign, Emma asked Thomas to spruce up the place some and provided him with a sizeable budget to make that happen. Deciding to take a more hands off approach, Emma and Cathy encouraged Thomas to use his own judgment in deciding what plants to purchase and where to place them. Thomas had a great eye and understanding of horticulture despite never having had any formal training. Everything he knew he learned from his late father who was a genius in his own right.

All of a sudden Tor came thundering through the kitchen with Poe following close behind. The sight made the group laugh. Little Poe was growing fast and had become a lot more steady on his young kitten legs. He'd taken to chasing Tor through the house when the opportunity presented itself.

Tor, for his part, appeared to enjoy the interaction. Little Poe liked wrestling with Tor and playfully attacking him. Tor fought back but knew his limits. When tiring of Poe's presence, he would jump to a higher elevation out of Poe's reach. Usually joining Emma on her section of the bench seat. Emma and Cathy were amazed by Tor's patience. Poe's constant clinging to and following Tor around made Cathy and Emma anxious but they admired his tolerance and acceptance of his new little sidekick. Still, they wondered how long Tor would put up with it before he let Poe have it. After all, they were well aware of Tor's hunting abilities. Fortunately, it was never a real concern. Tor loved the little kitten and often lavished him with affection when they were together.

Emma and Cathy still wouldn't let Poe hang out in the yard all day with Thomas. They felt he was still too small and worried a hawk or and owl might snatch him up. So mornings and evenings were especially exciting. Always happy to see each other again, Tor and Poe played for hours in Emma's house and then at Thomas's cottage until Thomas put Tor out for the night. This was the new routine and often proved to be great entertainment for all as they watched the two play.

Interrupted by the ringing of the kitchen phone, Emma excused herself to answer it. After Emma got up, Tor continued lying on the bench seat looking down at Poe.

Poe cried loudly attempting to jump and climb the side of the bench but the distance was too great. Looking at Tor with huge wide eyes, Poe cried defiantly, determined to get to his friend.

Cathy reached over and pet Tor. "Enjoy it while you can old fellow. Before long he'll be jumping up here with us."

"You can do it Mr. Poe, here, let me help you," Thomas said and lifted him onto the bench next to Tor. Poe immediately leapt on Tor with an affectionate embrace. Tail twitching, Tor looked at Thomas with an all too human disapproving look.

Cathy shook her head. "Sorry old fellow."

"Well, that was interesting," Emma said returning to the table. "It appears we're about to have a visitor."

"Really? Who?" Cathy asked.

"Devan is on his way over. He said he has some good news for me. I wonder what it could be?" she asked smiling.

"He's on his way over here? Now? This minute? Oh my God! He can't see me like this!" Cathy jumped from her seat. "I have to go change."

Emma looked at Thomas, "Like she has a chance." Thomas laughed.

"Oh shut up you two," Cathy said as she waved them off and headed to her room to change.

# # #

117

When Devan arrived, Cathy cheerfully greeted him at the door and showed him to the study where Emma was waiting. As Cathy left the room she pulled shut the two massive pocket doors closing off the room so they could speak in private. Gesturing for him to sit in a chair next to her, they both sat down.

"So, Devan. What's up?" she asked with her charismatic southern charm suspecting she already knew the answer.

Devan rarely divulged information over the phone. Knowing ears were constantly listening, he preferred instead to have face-to-face meetings and given the nature of his business, this was understandable. Little did people know, most of the time he had a signal jamming device on him capable of blocking phones and other recording devices. But, not this night. Emma was not his typical associate. Even though he still didn't really know her, he was confident she didn't present a threat.

"It turns out your suspicions about Pollock were right. He does answer to a higher power. John Douglas Sr. is the one pulling his strings," Devan answered.

"So it's the big prick, not the little one. Well now…that is interesting."

He couldn't help but smile at her comment.

"Did you find out why?" she asked.

"The mayor's father has big plans for that old warehouse complex and, until recently, your eight blocks. If his project goes forward, things are going to get very busy around here.

"Until recently? What changed?" Emma was not one to miss the obvious.

Devan's lips curled into a slight smile. "Let's just say I had a good conversation with John Sr. in my office earlier this evening and he's had a change of heart regarding those blocks. Instead, his primary focus now is on the warehouse complex and some new property adjoining it that recently became available."

"And our good Councilman Pollock?"

"I have a feeling you'll be hearing from him very soon," Devan said still holding his smile.

Dying to know all the details, Emma knew better and suppressed the urge to ask. Instead, she simply smiled back. "That is good news. Thank you for looking into this matter for us, Devan."

"It was my pleasure. And the offer of my assistant Cathy's help still stands. Even with Pollock on board, I think you'll find her very useful. She's had a lot of experience dealing with guys like him."

"I'd be delighted to have her help, thank you. And now that that business is out of the way, I'd be honored if you would join me and the gang in the kitchen for some cherry pie. Cathy makes the best cherry pie in the whole city and she just pulled one from the oven before you rang. It should be ready by now."

"How can I refuse an offer like that?" Devan asked standing to follow her to the kitchen.

The pie was indeed delicious. Cathy and Thomas had waited for Emma and were pleased to have Devan join them. Devan was humored by Tor as he watched him ravenously devour a small piece Cathy had given him. Discussing Thomas's recent plantings around the property, Thomas was especially excited to find out Devan had an extensive background in horticulture. Having considerable common ground, Devan and Thomas dominated the conversation talking about plants and techniques. Emma and Cathy mostly listened, but enjoyed watching Thomas interact with Devan so freely.

Finally noticing the time, Emma reminded Thomas of the late hour and suggested he give Devan a tour of the gardens one day in the near future. Before Devan could answer, Thomas excitedly suggested the next morning at 10:30. Devan could clearly see how much sharing the gardens meant to Thomas so he happily accepted. "Thanks Thomas. I'm looking forward to a personal tour." Devan looked at Emma and winked.

After Thomas said good night and left with Poe and Tor following close behind, Emma thanked Devan for being so kind to him. She told him this wasn't always the case with people. Many either ignored him or talked down to him like he was a small child.

As she and Cathy walked Devan out, Emma thanked him again for his help and agreeing to see the gardens with Thomas.

"I'll see you in the morning. Good night, ladies."

They watched him exit through the main gates. "So tell me. What did he say? Is Pollock going to help?" Cathy asked.

"He said he had a feeling Pollock will be giving us a call shortly."

"Really? I'll believe that when I see it."

"I have a hunch you wouldn't have to wait too long," Emma said as they walked back inside.

Chapter
22

After meeting with Devan, JD called his son as he drove home to share what he thought was good news.

"Look Jr., I don't want to argue about this. Getting the Port Authority property allows us to take this project to a whole new level. Now we have access to water front development and a whole lot more," JD said barely able to contain his excitement.

"I know father, but why can't we have both? We've already drawn up plans for developing those eight blocks. If we move quickly, I'm sure I can get enough residents to change their minds about that historical crap and sell. And for those who won't sell, we can use imminent domain to claim their property for official port use. After we clear everything, the Port Authority will change its mind and unload the property for nothing."

"No need, Jr.. Mr. Ross was very clear in that he wants those blocks to remain untouched and I agree. I'd rather focus on the new waterfront property and the warehouse complex. Let the residents have their historical district. In the end, it'll only help our cause."

"Who cares what Devan Ross wants? I'm the goddamn mayor! Why do we give a shit about him?" he demanded unable to control his frustration.

Not wanting to reveal what Devan had on him, JD instead reminded his son of how Devan helped him with his past drug situation. "Need I remind you, Jr., Mr. Ross was able to obtain and suppress that embarrassing video of you high and doing cocaine naked with those prostitutes at that sleazy hotel."

Always irritated when this was brought up, Jr. bristled. "How can I forget? Sometimes I think he set the whole thing up so he could hold it over my head for the rest of my life."

"A political life you wouldn't have for long in this town if that video ever became public. I didn't see him in that video. Only you, a lot of drugs and two whores. I don't know about you sonny, but that's some pretty incriminating shit. Fortunately, he was able to find your blackmailers and then make the whole thing go away."

"I know, but--"

"--Let it go, son. This is a good deal. And with Ross helping on the construction end, we're guaranteed to be successful."

"Devan Ross strikes again," the mayor said shaking his head. "Fine, father. It's your project," he said after a few moments of reflection.

"I knew you'd come around. And tell Pollock to play ball with the old lady. No more stalling. As a matter of fact, I think he should give her a call first thing in the morning."

The mayor was barely able to contain his mounting frustration. "I'll call him right now."

Hanging up the phone, the mayor sat at his desk in City Hall fuming. "Goddammit!" he blurted out loud. "Fuckin' Devan Ross and Emma Perkins!" Irritated, he did as he was instructed and called Pollock to give him his new marching orders.

"But, I thought you wanted me to stall the process?" Pollock asked.

"The situation has changed. Play ball with Mrs. Perkins and her friends. For now," he added.

"For now?" Pollock asked confused.

"Just do as you're told Pollock!" The mayor hung up the phone.

Councilman Pollock didn't know what to make of the short conversation, but a part of him was relieved he didn't have to dodge Emma anymore.

After hanging up with Pollock, the mayor sat at his desk stewing. Unknown to his father, he'd purchased several lots and homes throughout the eight blocks in question. Hoping to cash in on the future development, he'd over leveraged himself financially in order to acquire those properties.

Now, with his father shifting the project to the new property along the river, the realization of how screwed he was began to sink in.

Out of the depths of his despair, an idea began to take shape. Sitting up in his large chair, he twiddled his thumbs and smirked. "Sorry, Father. I just can't agree with you this time. I think there's a way for us to have our cake and eat it too," he said out loud. Reaching for the phone he made a call.

"Chase, it's me. We need to meet. I have an important task for you."

Chapter
23

Chase Carlton was the mayor's hired thug. Unknown to John Douglas Sr., but Chase had been lurking in his son's background for years. Not only did he serve as the mayor's current cocaine dealer, but when called on, was also his hired muscle. Multiple stints in various state prisons had hardened his character. Knowing there would never be a place for him in the legitimate world, Chase made a name for himself in other ways. Having met John Douglas Jr. years earlier, the two developed an unlikely relationship. John Jr. was a spoiled selfish child and grew to be an equally contemptable adult. Taking his privileged upbringing for granted, John Jr. viewed those around him as little more than subordinates. Never one to get his own hands dirty, John instead used others to do his dirty work for him. When he met Chase, Chase immediately sized up the situation and recognized an opportunity when he saw one. Being the primary hired hand to the son of one of the wealthiest families in the city was a golden opportunity he wasn't going to pass up.

Meeting at a familiar bar in Riverside, Chase waited in a dark corner booth. He didn't have to wait long. After joining him, the mayor immediately got down to business. "I have a big problem and I need your help."

Chase remained quiet. He casually took a healthy swig from his beer. "What do you need?"

"That old bag Emma Perkins is leading a drive to get the remaining eight blocks in East Springfield protected with a historical designation. If that happens, I'll lose my ass."

"I thought your father's company was going to develop that area?"

"He was until she started her movement and got Devan Ross involved. Now father plans to go another direction and not use the eight blocks at all." He tapped the table with his knuckles. Irritated.

Chase knew this was bad news for the mayor. Over the past year and at the mayor's request, Chase had been leaning on and out right threatening property owners to sell at greatly reduced prices. Through a web of fake companies, John Jr. bought the properties – some commercial, some residential homes. He'd hoped to cash in big when the development began. He quietly leveraged most of his and his wife's assets to acquire these properties. He hoped this would finally allow him to make some real money of his own. Though he was a grown man with a family, he still held tightly to his father's purse strings. Technically, when he became mayor he divested himself of all connections to his family's business, but the reality was, his father was still very much calling the shots.

Chase sat up showing more interest. "Devan Ross? How the hell did he get dragged into this?" he asked.

"I have no idea. Somehow he and Perkins have become friends. It was Ross that got my old man to change his mind about the eight blocks."

Knowing Devan Ross was involved changed things. Crossing paths with him was not an encounter Chase wanted. He remained quiet for a moment. "I don't like Ross being involved."

"Oh, for Christ's sake! You too? You're afraid of him, too?"

Chase's cold, black eyes locked on the mayor. Fixed in his empty stair, John Jr. went silent. Chase didn't like being mocked by anyone, especially privileged assholes like the one sitting across from him. His look made this very clear to the mayor.

"Ok, look, I don't want to tangle with him either. It's the Perkins woman I need dealt with. I need her to go away, somehow. I'm sure once she's out of the picture Ross will lose interest."

"What are you proposing?" Chase asked taking another swig of his beer.

"I was thinking maybe you could use your considerable arson skills to make Mrs. Perkins and the beloved Carson House disappear forever. If it looks like a tragic accident, the whole thing will blow over and that loose coalition of residents will most likely fall apart. Then, I'm sure I can convince my father to move in and buy the remaining properties with little opposition."

Chase was quiet; thinking to himself. Finally, "What's in it for me?" he asked. John Jr. was waiting for it. He leaned in and lowered his voice to nearly a whisper. "If we're successful silencing Mrs. Perkins, you'll have more money than you'll know what to do with."

Chase nodded. "Give me a week or so to study the situation and I'll get back to you with my answer."

The mayor knew this was a typical Chase response. He was never one to immediately agree to anything - he liked to weigh his options. In this case, he needed to do some reconnaissance in order to see how feasible the mayor's plan was.

Chase had an extensive arson background. He was often employed by business and homeowners to destroy property by fire in a way that looked like a legitimate accident. But the Mayor's plan was more complicated. Not only would he have to make this fire look like an accident, but he'd also have to make sure Emma Perkins perished as well.

Chapter
24

As promised, Councilman Pollock called Emma the following morning. After making his apologies for not getting back to her sooner, he explained how busy he had been, but now had more time to devote to helping her and his constituents. Emma was gracious, as usual, and shared with him the progress she, Councilwoman Danfora, and the others had made. She also invited him to a meeting that was taking place in a few weeks where she, Councilwoman Danfora, and other community leaders were planning to host a question and answer session with the residents and property owners of the blocks in question before they voted either to go forward with pursuing the historical designation or not. Pollock enthusiastically agreed to attend and told her he looked forward to seeing her then offered to help where he could. He also wanted her to know she had his full support in this matter. When Emma hung up the phone she shook her head and said out loud, "Politicians! Nothing but bottom dwellers and bullshit artists."

Chapter 25

Chase may not have had a formal education or military background, but what he did know, he knew well and arson was his specialty. Over his lifetime, he had perfected the art of making a fire appear accidental even to the best arson investigators. For Chase, arson was the family business.

Raised in Detroit, Chase's father supported the family by doing arson jobs for a wide range of clients. As the Detroit inner city declined, property owners found other ways to cash-in on their derelict and abandoned properties - insurance fires. And Chase's father was among the most notorious. He had a talent for his craft. Banks, investment companies, private individuals, even politicians discretely requested his help. For many, it was cheaper to cash-in through an insurance claim than to renovate or rebuild. But, as insurance fraud grew in popularity, so did the investigations. Having to pay out millions of dollars in claims, the insurance companies fought back. By changing arson coverage and hiring the best investigators using the latest arson detection technology, the insurance companies eliminated the rash of fraudulent fires almost overnight. Most amateur arsonists were forced out of business immediately. Chase's father, on the other hand, saw an opportunity. Perfecting his art, he studied the detection techniques and found cleaver ways to beat them.

Chase's father had no respect for the laws of society. Orphaned, he'd been forced to find ways to survive his entire life, he knew no other path. At an early age he got his son involved in the family business. Not because he loved him and wanted to teach him a trade, but because he was small and could fit into tight places he could not. Since Chase's mother left when he was only seven, there was nobody to discourage this. At age 12, Chase was still small in stature, but hard as nails. Having perfected the art of the accidental fire, his father grew to depend on his son's ability to wiggle into tight spaces. Even though his father rarely acknowledged Chase's own talents and abilities, he knew he couldn't do what he did without his help. Seeing no need for a formal education, his father encouraged him to drop out of school in the ninth grade. For the next three years the two traveled the country at the request of clients. The money was good, but his father drank to excess. Between the booze, prostitutes, and drugs, they went through their earnings fast. Fortunately, there was always another job to be had somewhere.

When Chase was seventeen, his father took a job in Portland, Oregon. The plan was to destroy a townhouse in a protected historical area of town. The present owner wanted to tear it down but after months of opposition by preservation groups, he finally agreed to restore the building. But as the expenses began to add up, it was clear to the owner that it was a money pit. Not wanting to reignite the public controversy, he sought out other professionals. The kind skilled at making these kinds of problems go away.

Suffering from a lifetime of injuries and poor health, Chase's father had developed a strong dependence on pain medications. Not one for going to the doctor, he choose to self-medicate. Smoking pot was his first choice, but as age caught up with him he moved on to stronger substitutes. Heroin was now his drug of choice. Supporting his drug habit required more sources of income and often became a major point of contention between the two. Out of necessity, Chase added robbery as arson was no longer paying all the bills. Still slim by nature, the streets and his father's abusiveness had hardened him. Now six feet tall and all muscle, Chase could take care of himself if he had to.

The night they were supposed to set the fire in the Oregon townhouse, his father got high and became useless. Having already done all the prep work and knowing they only had the one night to get this done thanks to a holiday, Chase was furious. Leaving his father passed out in their hotel room, he decided to do the job himself. Using undetectable devices to provide ignition as well as chemicals impossible to detect, Chase set the scene, making it look like old wiring started the blaze. Pleased with his work, he set the timers and returned to the hotel. But to his surprise, his father was gone.

Suddenly remembering the townhome, he raced out. By the time he got to the building, it was already engulfed in flames. Fire crews were swarming the scene. Seeing a person being loaded into an ambulance, Chase approached. The body on the gurney was unrecognizable. Severely burned, Chase recoiled with horror. "Dad?" he asked. It was all he could manage to say looking on at the distorted figure convulsing in excruciating pain.

"Do you know this man?" a paramedic asked.

Quickly realizing his predicament, Chase shook his head and disappeared into the crowd.

"Wait! Come back!" the paramedic shouted. He told a police officer, but it was too late. Chase had fled. He returned to the hotel, gathered all his personal belongings and took off. From that night Chase had been on his own.

# # #

Walking along the sidewalk, Chase occasionally stopped and looked through the vegetation growing through the rod iron fencing. Occasionally there was a break and he could get a clear view of Carson House. Having been built in the early 1900's, he knew there was ample fuel for a fire. When he noticed a gas meter on the side of the house, he smiled.

"This is almost too easy," he said out loud looking through the fence.

Rounding a corner and facing the house from another street, he was able to get another view of the property through a small opening in the dense vegetation. He could see a large black man raking leaves off a thick mat of healthy green grass. He also noticed a black and white cat looking in his direction. For a second it looked like the cat was looking right at him. He walked a little farther down the sidewalk and found another small opening to look through. Again, he saw the black man. But more puzzling, the cat had turned and was facing his direction. Walking back down the sidewalk to his original point of view from the corner, he looked through the vegetation. The cat was gone.

Chase continued his walk around the block and down another sidewalk. When he reached a break in the fencing next to a large steel gate he was surprised to find the cat sitting there waiting for him.

"What are you looking at, cat?" He said and pretended to jump at him.

Tor did not budge. He looked like a statue. He sat motionless staring at Chase with intense yellow-green eyes. If it wasn't for the occasional agitated twitch of his tail, one would think he was a statue.

"I said, what are you looking at?"

Tor's eyes ignited into a fiery yellow glow. At the same time he hissed and growled at Chase and began moving in his direction like he was going to attack.

"What the fuck?" Chase jumped back off the sidewalk and almost into the path of an approaching bus.

"Where are you, Mr. Tor? It's time for lunch," Thomas shouted looking around for the cat.

When Chase recovered and looked through the opening again he saw Tor following Thomas. Abruptly, Tor stopped and turned looking directly at him. Cautiously, Chase backed away from the fence and continued down the sidewalk.

"Come on Mr. Tor. Poe's going to eat all your food," Thomas joked with him.

Tor trotted behind Thomas into the house.

#

After leaving Emma's, Chase called the Mayor. On the second ring he answered.

"I checked out the problem and have an idea. I need a week or so to get everything I'll need to do the job," Chase said.

"That's cutting it close. Just make sure it's done before the city council meeting three weeks from now."

"Don't worry, Mr. Mayor. I can assure you this problem will go up in smoke long before that meeting."

Chapter
26

The next two weeks were busy for everyone. Cindy did not disappoint. As Devan promised, she was a force to be reckoned with. Getting right to work, she had Pollock jumping over hurdles and through hoops like a trained circus animal. Emma loved it. They even contacted Ryan Anderson, the young man who brought Tor home after the fight and enlisted his help in putting together a small advertising campaign to spread awareness and information. Though well below the level of the typical campaign Ryan worked on, he was honored to devote his time to their cause. Councilwoman Danfora and the other members of the residential and historical societies also provided assistance when call upon. With everyone now on the same page, progress was being made fast in preparation for the final residential community meeting and vote scheduled to take place a few days away.

Planning to host the meeting at Carson House, Thomas had been hard at work landscaping. The grounds were beautiful. So much so, Emma, Councilman Pollock, and Councilwoman Danfora hosted several lower key events at Emma's in preparation for the main event. Thomas' work spoke for itself and visitors frequently commented on how beautiful the grounds were. Using Carson House as a focal point, it shined brightly as an example of what other homes in the area could one day become.

Chapter
27

On the morning of the final community meeting and vote, the mayor called Pollock.

"But Mr. Mayor, I'm supposed to be there. I can't not go," Pollock stressed into the phone not believing what John Jr. was telling him to do.

There was a long awkward silence that made Pollock feel even more uncomfortable.

"Of course you can. Remember why you have your job. We put you in that councilman seat for exactly this reason. Ross and Emma Perkins have made a huge mess of this whole deal. If that historical designation is approved, we're fucked. It'll cost me a fortune! So right now your only job is to buy time."

"Time? Time for what? They don't need me. Emma has been working with Danfora."

"Yes, but they need you to bring the historical request to the city council for a vote since it's in your district and that cannot be allowed to happen."

Perspiring heavily and frantically twirling the phone cord in his fingers, Pollock was stressing. Right now he hated his job. At first it was easy. He had the smallest district and it was largely industrial. The Douglas family owned most of the property. What businesses were in his district were small and the residents rarely asked for anything. In order to make sure their current and future business interests were protected, the Douglas family bought a councilman seat. Pollock was an obedient flunky selected from a field of useless middle management in the family's corporate headquarters in Jacksonville. "Big Daddy", John Douglas Sr. himself, approached Pollock and presented his offer. Agreeing to fully fund his run for office as well as furnish a lavish residence conveniently located within the district along with a generous increase in salary, Pollock jumped at the offer. In return for this generosity, when the family needed something Pollock would be their direct line to the city council as well as serve as the family's eyes and ears. For the most part, the job was easy. Pollock flew under the radar by design. He earned political points by helping other council members which allowed him to amass a considerable number of IOUs. For years, Pollock played his part well and enjoyed his low-key existence, always maneuvering behind the scenes.

When the Douglas family made their Springfield development plans known to him, he was excited. Knowing the development would be huge, he looked forward to the project and even purchased several properties he hoped to sell at a much higher price once the news was out. That was until Devan Ross entered the picture. Ross' reputation worried him greatly. It was rumored that behind Ross' public face was something entirely different. For reasons unknown to him, the city's movers and shakers gave him a wide berth. He had heard rumors, but knew few facts. Even the Douglas family treaded lightly where Ross was concerned – often going out of their way to not cross his path. This concerned Pollock the most. He felt like they were using him to distract Ross while they plotted and planned in the background. He knew the family was annoyed by Emma and hated that she was spearheading the historical movement. Pollock felt if Ross and Emma Perkins hadn't established such a good friendship, the family might have taken steps to silence Mrs. Perkins a long time ago. But now, having him lie and deliberately mislead Ross and Mrs. Perkins for weeks was rattling his nerves. The mayor was using him for his own personal gain. What the hell am I doing? he thought to himself. How did I get into this mess? He knew it was just a matter of time before he was going to be squashed by one side or the other. Trembling, helpless and looking for a way out, Pollock made a desperate suggestion.

"Sir, I want to resign my position as councilman. I...I think someone else would do a better job."

The mayor was silent for an uncomfortable few seconds. "Do you? I'd think long and hard on that before making any hasty decisions." The mayor hung up. Pollock sat at his desk holding the phone hearing nothing but silence. Shaking uncontrollably, he barely managed to put the phone back on the receiver.

# # #

Sitting at his desk the mayor picked up his phone and dialed a number. A voice answered on the second ring.

"What?"

"Chase?"

"Yeah?"

"It's time."

"When?"

"As soon as you're ready."

"Consider it done."

"But first I need you to pay a visit to Councilman Pollock's office. It seems he wants to quit. I'd like you to persuade him to change his mind."

The line went dead. John Jr. calmly hung up the phone. "You may be a quitter, Father, but I'm not," he said out loud.

Chapter
28

Realizing at the last minute how many people were planning to attend the final residential meeting and vote, Councilwoman Danfora arranged to have a meeting hall booked instead of Emma's home. If the residents voted in favor of pursuing the historical designation, Councilman Pollock would formally take the request to the city council the following week. Once they agreed to the request, then the measure moved on to the state and federal level. If approved, this opened the door for state and federal grants as well as new construction, preservation, and rehab loans to all residents living in or owing property in the designated area. The residents would also qualify for a wide variety of tax deductions and other incentives. The catch was that the homes had to be maintained in original and period appropriate condition when viewed from the street. This was important to understand because it did impose restrictions on what property owners could do to their homes without permission from an oversite committee. It was also important for the residents to understand what kind of consequences they might face if they violated the agreement.

As people began to arrive, it quickly became obvious it had been a good idea to move the meeting to the larger venue. With all the attention being focused on the area, attendance was the highest yet. Devan's personal assistant Cindy, had been helping Emma and Councilwoman Danfora prepare for days. Emma and Cindy bonded instantly. Devan gave her unlimited leave to help Emma in any capacity needed. Emma quickly realized why Devan had so much confidence in her. Cindy's ability to organize and execute strategy reminded her of her younger Navy days. Jon and Angie Smith were also there to help field questions as well as members from relevant state and federal agencies. But it was Emma who was the real star. Having championed the cause for months, she was the face most associated with the movement.

The meeting was scheduled for 11:00a.m. The venue was full of residents and other property owners anxiously waiting for the meeting to start. Cindy walked into the staging room off the main hall a little past 11:00 and shrugged her shoulders. "What's the plan? Are we going to do this thing or what?"

"What about Mr. Pollock?" Cathy asked looking around. "Doesn't he have to be here?"

"He's probably passed out in a bar someplace. Let's get this show on the road. If Pollock shows great, if not, it's his loss," Emma said. Eager to get started, she led the group to the stage.

The meeting was scheduled for one hour and then the residents would vote either for or against moving forward with the historical designation. However, the meeting could be extended if it was decided more time was needed to hear from concerned residents. After the initial presentations, the floor was open to questions. Emma and the others were honest and as open as possible. They were determined to present all the information so people could make informed decisions. Amazingly, Emma fielded most of the questions having been well coached by Cindy. The others helped where needed but for the most part it was Emma's show.

At 12:30p.m., a vote was called and by 1:00p.m., all residents had cast their ballots. It took another hour to count the votes. By 2:00p.m., they had a final tally. Overwhelmingly, the residents voted in favor of moving forward with pursuing the historical designation. Delighted by the results, Emma and Councilwoman Danfora hung around for another hour answering any lingering questions and concerns people might have. Finally, by 3:00p.m., Cindy stepped in and officially wrapped things up. More than once Cindy was impressed by Emma's energy and stamina. On her way back to the office Cindy called Devan to give him the good news and a quick rundown of the day's events. It was agreed that it was probably better Devan not attend the meeting since he was associated with one of the largest construction firms in northeast Florida. His presence might be seen as suspicious by some. When Devan answered, he was eager to hear what Cindy had to report.

Chapter 29

"What do you mean Pollock never showed?" Devan said standing up from his desk. "That little prick was supposed to be there. You're telling me he was a no show?" Devan barked at the speaker phone on his desk.

"Yes, sir. He never showed up. Emma covered for him and if you ask me, she did a much better job. She and Councilwoman Danfora fielded most of the questions from the audience. What they couldn't answer was handled by the others. Despite him being a no show, I think the meeting went very well. The majority of residents voted in favor of moving forward with the measure. Emma even stayed and talked with residents long after the votes had been tallied and posted. It's hard to believe she's in her eighties," Cindy said. She was slowly making her way through the afternoon traffic on her way back to the office.

"Emma is quite a woman. Thanks for helping out. I'll see you when you get back. Drive safely."

"It was my pleasure. You know I always enjoy my visits with Mrs. Perkins."

"You are two peas in a pod."

After hanging up, Devan leaned back in his chair and shook his head. Pollock's behavior had reached its limits. At first, Devan tolerated it knowing he was a drunk. Fortunately, he and Emma just needed him to stay out of the way until called on. But after missing today's meeting, it was obvious Pollock's strings were still being pulled by someone and Devan was determined to find out who. That little shit has fucked up for the last time. Time to pay him a visit myself.

Chapter
30

Pollock heard a knock on his open door and looked up to see Chase standing in the doorway. Immediately he sat up. "What are you doing here?"

Entering the office, Chase slowly shut the door and locked it. "The boss sent me to have a talk with you." He pulled a set of brass knuckles from his pocket and put them on his right hand. "Now we can do this easy or hard. It really doesn't matter to me," Chase said with a twisted psychotic smile.

#

Pollock's assistant, Melony Ferguson, returned from a late afternoon doctor's appointment a few minutes after Chase entered Pollock's office. She had no idea he had company. Hearing a violent commotion coming from inside, she ran to the door and tried to open it only to find it locked. "Mr. Pollock! Are you ok, sir?" she asked frantically knocking on the door.

"Yes, I'm fine. Go back to what you were doing," he responded not opening the door. Melony stood at the door for a few moments then did as instructed.

A short time later Chase walked out. When he passed by her desk, he winked at her making her skin crawl.

#

Devan was no stranger to City Hall. Over the years he'd been there many times for one reason or another. Pollock had a small office at the end of a long hall on the third floor. Taking Jamison with him made for an intimidating sight – the exact reaction Devan wanted.

"So why are we going to see this guy?" Jamison asked as they ascended in the elevator.

"Pollock's been dodging Emma again. Missing the meeting and vote today was the last straw. Somethings up with him and I'm determined to get to the bottom of it. And you my friend are a scary fellow."

"You're using me to scare this dude?" Jamison asked frowning.

"Yep. Old school."

"How do you know it'll work?"

"Well, you scare the hell out of me, so I figure this guy doesn't stand a chance," Devan said slapping his shoulder as they exited the elevator on Pollock's floor.

"Good to know, Boss."

Truth be known, it was Devan who was feared by most. But, not by Jamison. If anything, he had the deepest respect for Devan. Having given him a chance when so many others wouldn't, he was fiercely loyal and protective of his boss and friend.

Walking down the hall, Devan noticed a rough looking man exiting Pollock's office in the distance. Something about the guy got his attention. He had a scar on his right cheek and dark, cold eyes. Devan and Jamison did their best to stay to one side of the hall, but both were large men. When the guy passed, he didn't attempt to avoid them and intentionally didn't move. Devan turned slightly to avoid contact, but Jamison did not. When the guy hit him it was like hitting a wall, Jamison gave no ground. Neither looked back and kept going to Pollock's office. The hit was intentional. Devan couldn't help but smile. He knew Jamison would do that.

When they reached Pollock's office, his assistant seemed visibly shaken. Recognizing her and also noticing her unsettled demeanor, Devan figured it had something to do with the guy who just left. "Melony? What's going on?" he asked.

"Devan! What are you doing here?" she asked surprised and trying to be professional. Melony was a familiar visitor to his San Marco night club, The Vault. Devan had also helped her deal with a stalker ex-boyfriend several years ago at the request of Melony's older sister, his current club manager.

"We're here to see Mr. Pollock," Devan said. Jamison stood next to him with his arms crossed.

"I'm sorry, but Mr. Pollock isn't seeing visitors right now. If you'd like to make an appointment, I can reschedule you for another day," she said still flustered.

"I think today will do," Devan said walking by her and right into Pollock's office. When he entered he was stopped in his tracks. Pollock was disheveled, shirt partly untucked and had a bruised and bloody lip. Jamison and Melony followed.

They were all momentarily stunned. "Mr. Pollock, what happened?" Melony asked.

"Nothing. I slipped and fell hitting my desk. I'll be ok," he replied stuttering. It was obvious he was trying to down play the incident.

"I'm sorry to bother you, sir, but Mr. Ross insisted on seeing you."

Recognizing Devan immediately and seeing Jamison caused his heart to sink. Trying to hide his building fear he managed to stay calm. "It's ok, Melony, I'll see them. That'll be all."

After she left, he motioned toward two chairs that had been knocked over and then gestured for them to sit down.

Devan and Jamison righted the chairs and sat. "I see I'm not the only one you have trouble with today," Devan said trying to lighten the atmosphere. Pollock's quivering lip and shaking body were not missed by either man. Jamison locked eyes on him.

"I don't know what you mean," Pollock said unconvincing.

"Don't bullshit me Pollock. You've been dragging your ass in helping Emma and I'm not leaving here until I find out why." Jamison leaned forward, but said nothing.

Fearing another beating, Pollock snapped. "Because I was told not to help you!" he blurted out in a panic.

"By who?" Devan demanded.

"The mayor. He told me not to help - to draw it out as long as possible."

"But why? I already talked to his father. We had a deal. He assured me this would not be a problem. Are you telling me he lied?" Devan's question was more a demand and Pollock almost broke down crying.

"No! Not JD. John Jr. He thinks his father was wrong in scaling back the project. John Jr. insists on including the eight blocks. He feels reconfiguring the development will cost them millions. He wants me to delay bringing the request to the council."

"Sorry to disappoint you, but as of now I'm here to inform you that you will be doing just that and you'll be doing it at next week's council meeting. Do I make myself clear?" Devan asked. "I don't know what you and his Honor the Idiot have going on, but it's over. Even JD agrees this is the right move."

Pollock held his head and leaned over his desk. "I don't want to do this anymore. I tried to quit today, but the mayor sent that goon in to rough me up. He won't let me go. Please, I just want out of this."

Devan looked at Jamison then back to Pollock. "You have a choice. You can join my team, the winning team, or you can stay with the mayor's sinking ship. John Jr. is not getting those eight blocks. Do I make myself clear?"

Pollock nodded his head in agreement.

"Then we agree you will bring the request to the council so they can vote on the measure?"

Pollock nodded. "I'll do it, but you know he won't like it."

"Good. I'll deal with John Jr.," Devan said in a cool confident tone.

As they left Pollock's office, they were being watched. Recognizing Devan, Chase decided to hang around to see what was going on. Remaining unseen, he hid in a cubical complex where he had a good view of the office. He saw Devan and Pollock shake hands when they walked out and heard Pollock thank Devan for his help. The mood appeared light and friendly.

"So, the little shit sold out," he said to himself. "I'll be seeing you very soon, Councilman."

Chapter

31

After leaving City Hall, Chase called the mayor. "Looks like we have a complication," Chase said when he answered.

"What?"

"It appears Pollock sold out. I just saw him and Devan Ross shaking hands together outside his office. The two looked pretty friendly to me."

"Fucking Ross! Damn him!" The mayor pounded his desk.

"I have an idea about how to handle this, but I'm not going to talk about it over the phone. Meet me in Riverside in 30 minutes. We could both use a drink," Chase said.

# # #

The mayor joined Chase in the dark corner booth at their regular rendezvous location in Riverside.

"What's your idea?" asked John Jr.

"How attached are you to Councilman Pollock?" Chase asked fixing his ice cold eyes on John Jr. followed by an uncharacteristic smile.

Chase's plan was to have the mayor call Pollock and tell him to meet him at Devan's club the following evening. He was to tell him they worked everything out and he wanted to discuss moving forward. Pollock would show, but the mayor would not. After letting Pollock hang out and be seen for a little while, he'd receive another call telling him to meet somewhere else a lot more secluded. Once alone, Chase would abduct him and that would be the last anyone ever saw of Mr. Pollock. After disposing of his body, he would take care of Emma. Chase would plant incriminating arson evidence at Pollock's home linking him to the fire at Emma's. Chase even suggested tying Devan to Pollock in an attempt to link him to the crime. If they were lucky, linking Devan to a missing councilman and the deliberate burning of Carson House would destroy his reputation and at last remove him from the top of the Jacksonville power structure.

"We might actually kill three birds with one stone. Brilliant idea. Tomorrow night it is. No more Emma Perkins and no more Devan Ross."

John Jr. raised his glass and clinked Chase's beer bottle.

Chapter
32

Friday nights at both of Devan's clubs were always busy, but The Vault, was usually the more popular with a wider variety of people. When one entered through two sets of huge double glass front doors, they entered into an open two-story dance club with a massive glass ceiling overhead. A long bar lit with a neon red light dominated half of one side of the room. Directly opposite the front door on the other side of the room was a raised stage for bands or additional dance space. Recessed booths and tables were strategically spread throughout the space, but more to the right. The center was open dance space. A grand staircase elegantly curved up the wall to the right connecting the second story to the first or guests could use either of two glass elevators to move between the floors. Once upstairs, one side of the room had a similar but smaller bar like the one down below. Tables, booths and recessed lounging areas were spread throughout. Because of the way the acoustics were planned, one could be sitting in any of the lounging areas and still be able to have a conversation. But, once out on the dance floor, the music dominated.

Next to the ground floor bar was a wide hallway leading to another elevator at the end. In a more secluded room off this hallway and behind the large bar was the bank's original vault. It had been converted into a storage area for high end liquors from around the world. Kept at a constant temperature below freezing, tours were conducted of its contents nightly. Sampling these different liquors was offered at a premium. Even though the price was high, since the clubs opening, there hadn't been a night they didn't have a wait list hours long. Touring the vault and sampling its contents had become a must do among Jacksonville's elite for over a decade.

Off to the left of the hallway was an exclusive reservations-only restaurant. It never tried to be the best in the city, but most claimed it was. Like the vault bar, reservations were often booked weeks out. At the end of the hallway, the elevator lead to the roof and a revolving glass bar and restaurant with a limited menu. It turned at one revolution per hour. The rooftop bar and premier downstairs restaurant could also be accessed through private entrances so one would not have to enter through the larger club. The second floor above the restaurant and vault bar were Devan's main offices and only accessible by a separate elevator manned 24/7 by his private security detail.

After receiving the mayor's phone call earlier in the day, Pollock arrived at the club at 8:00p.m. as instructed. He went upstairs and took a seat at the smaller bar where he immediately ordered a drink. The mayor had assured him things had been worked out between him and his father. He invited Pollock out to apologize for how he treated him and wanted them to meet so they could discuss moving forward together. Pollock accepted the mayor's invitation. He hated being in the predicament he was in and looked forward to putting everything behind them.

After an hour at the bar, Pollock was pretty drunk. To be respectful to the mayor, he had turned off his phone. When the mayor called to change the location, he couldn't reach Pollock. Blissfully unaware he was trying to be reached by the mayor, Pollock continued drinking.

The mayor called Chase.

"I can't get a hold of Pollock. He's not answering his phone – I've been trying for half an hour. The dumbass won't pick up. I can't go in there and be seen, it'll ruin everything."

Chase and his accomplice, Dallas Cooper, had been waiting in a dark parking lot around the block from Devan's building. Like the mayor, and even Devan, Chase had a crew of loyal associates. Dallas was his number one man. They'd already shot out several street lights with a high-powered silent pellet gun as well as two security cameras on buildings facing their selected staging areas. They felt confident nobody would be able to see what took place in the shadows now. "Ok, I'll go," Chase said. "I'll tell him you're outside and want to meet somewhere else."

"Good. Call me when it's done."

# # #

Recognizing a familiar face at the bar, Melony, Pollock's assistant, greeted him affectionately.

"How nice it is to see you, sir. I thought that was you when I came up the stairs."

Very drunk, Pollock almost fell out of his chair when he turned to greet her.

"Melony? Melony!" he said again recognizing her. "Hey there, young lady. How are you?" He slurred asking the question.

Realizing he was quite drunk, Melony remained friendly but also wanted to get away as soon as she could. "I'm great. This is my regular hang out. My sister manages the club," she said making polite conversation, but doubted he heard her, he seemed fixated on his watch.

"Oh, that's nice honey. Can you tell me what time it is? I was supposed to meet someone at 8." He had managed to say that a lot clearer than she thought possible.

"It's after nine sir. Who were you meeting?" she asked out of curiosity.

He put his finger to his lips. "I can't tell you. It's a secret. He told me not to tell anyone who I was meeting." He winked and took another swig of his drink.

"Ok, Mr. Pollock. If that's the case, then I'll leave you to it. Hope your friend shows soon. Goodnight, sir," she said and disappeared into the crowd. Curious, she casually kept an eye on him from a booth across the room where she joined her friends.

# # #

It didn't take Chase long to find Pollock. Seeing him at the bar, he walked over.

From her vantage point across the room Melony immediately recognized Chase. Even though he wore a hat and looked as if he was purposely trying to disguise himself, she recognized him.

Chase greeted Pollock in a friendly manor. Even adding to the deception he apologized to Pollock for what he did to him in his office and asked for his forgiveness. He said he was only following orders. He even extended his hand to shake.

Pollock, very drunk, accepted his apology and shook his hand. Chase told him the mayor was outside and wanted to invite him to accompany them to a quieter venue. When they got up to leave, Chase told Pollock he needed to use the restroom and would meet him in the parking lot behind the club. The truth was, Chase wanted to exit out another door so if video was pulled, he wouldn't be seen leaving with him.

Melony noticed the two men leave together and decided to follow them for the heck of it. After what she witnessed in Pollock's office the day before, she had reason to be concerned. She watched as Pollock exited out the back entrance by the rooftop elevator and noticed Chase leave through the main front entrance. Melony quickly followed Pollock making sure to remain out of sight. She followed him through the parking lot. When he reached the darkened lot behind the building, she saw Chase approach. He pointed to a car across the street parked in a heavily shadowed lot. Using other vehicles for cover, she moved closer. All of a sudden another man appeared out of the darkness throwing a thin cord around Pollock's neck and pulling it tight. After a brief struggle, Pollock fell to the ground in a lifeless crumpled heap. Chase and Dallas quickly loaded him into the trunk of the parked car. Horrified, Melony remained still, petrified with fear holding her hands to her mouth.

"That takes care of Pollock. Next we deal with the Perkins bitch and then last but not least, the mighty Mr. Devan Ross himself," Chase said, addressing his associate. "But first, I have to call the boss and let him know Pollock's been taken care of.

After they drove off, Melony passed out from shock. Collapsing beside the truck she was hiding behind, she wasn't visible to club guests as they passed by.

Chapter
33

"Good night, Mr. Tor. Get some sleep. We have a busy day tomorrow," Thomas said letting Tor out for the night. Thomas had indeed been busy with his landscaping projects. Even though they shifted the historical meeting and vote to the larger venue, Emma still wanted Thomas to continue with his landscaping plans. She had already hosted several informal meetings at her home and planned to have many more as things moved forward. Carson House, had become more than Emma's home. It was now a powerful focal point as well as a shining example of what the area once was and could be again.

Tor sat on Thomas's patio bathing himself for a few minutes before beginning his nightly routine. Making his way to the hidden opening in the wall, he cautiously peered out. Even though it was a Friday night, the streets in this part of Springfield were practically deserted. Most of the residents had long since turned in for the evening. Feeling comfortable it was safe, he emerged onto the sidewalk. Pausing for a minute, he smelled the warm night air before heading off in the direction of the warehouse complex.

# # #

After taking care of Pollock and loading him into their trunk, Chase drove toward Emma's. Having been observing Emma's house nightly for over a week, he felt pretty comfortable he had their routine down. It was a little after 10:00pm and he knew in another hour or so, the house would be asleep.

"What are we going to do with Pollock's body?" Dallas asked.

"After we take care of the old woman, we're going to dispose of it. We need Pollock to disappear – he can't be found. It'll look more suspicious this way. Then we're going to his house to plant evidence linking him to Devan Ross. The mayor and I already created some realistic printouts of emails between Pollock and Ross discussing his betrayal of the historical society and Ross' desire to purchase the eight blocks in question."

"Why the printouts?" Dallas asked.

"We wanted it to look like Pollock was collecting his own evidence on Ross to protect himself. We also set Pollock up for the fire that's going to destroy Carson House by having him suggest taking out Mrs. Perkins and burning her house down. We made Pollock the arsonist doing Ross' bidding. This way we can be sloppy, we want fire investigators to find evidence of arson. With the evidence and no Pollock, it'll look like Pollock took off and left Ross to face the fire so to speak. It might not be enough to lock Ross up, but it'll damn sure give him a black eye in the community," Chase said, confident of his plan.

It didn't take long to reach Emma's. Chase circled the block a few times checking out the house. It was 10:30p.m., and with the exception of two porch lights, the house was dark.

"Just like clockwork," Chase said satisfied everyone had already turned in for the night. He found a deserted side alley between two buildings across the street and parked. To be safe, they decided to wait until 11:00. They wanted to be sure everyone was sound asleep when they entered the house.

# # #

Friday nights for Tor were not as satisfying as other week day nights. Garbage pick-up for the sandwich shop dumpster was Friday and the shop wasn't open on weekends so the amount of trash in the dumpster to attract rats and mice was minimal. Still, being the experienced hunter he was, he exercised patience. Having already made one kill, he was looking for a second before returning home. Waiting motionless on top of a concrete wall, Tor sat scanning the alley for any sign of movement.

# # #

When the pale green numbers of the car's clock change to 11:00p.m., Chase looked at Dallas. "Let's do this."

Dallas nodded in agreement. They exited the car and made their way across the street, both carrying backpacks containing everything they would need to break in and set the fire. They stayed in the shadows making their way along the wall to where limbs from a large tree inside the compound grew low over the fence and sidewalk. Just out of reach, Dallas threw a rope over the lowest limb securing it; Chase climbed up and Dallas followed. They pulled the rope up and left it in the tree so it wouldn't be seen.

"First we have to take care of the idiot gardener," Chase said pointing in the direction of Thomas's cottage.

When they reached the cottage they noticed there was a light on above the door. Chase smashed the bulb with a small metal club he pulled from his backpack then rang the doorbell frantically.

Thomas abruptly woke up hearing the bell ringing. He quickly ran to the door and looked out the small peephole but didn't see anyone since it was dark. "Who is it?" he asked. He was tired, but alert.

"Sir, I'm with the fire department. There's been an accident. The lady of the house sent me to get you," Chase said. He stood off to one side of the door, Dallas was on the other.

Concerned and panicked, Thomas opened the door and stepped out.

Chase smashed him on the back of his head and neck with the pipe, knocking him to the ground. Dallas kicked and punched him. Still trying to get up, Chase hit him again and again. Finally Thomas collapsed unconscious.

"He's still breathing," Dallas said hearing ragged breaths.

"Good. If he lives, he'll tell people he got jumped. If he dies, that works too. Come on, let's get to the old ladies and light this candle." They sprinted up the path toward the house.

Chapter
34

Sitting motionless on the wall waiting for his prey, Tor suddenly felt uneasy. A bad feeling came over him. Something was wrong. He leapt to the ground and stood motionless. Again he felt it, and again. The nightly hunt was over. Time to go home. He shot down the alley and out into the warehouse complex as fast as he could.

# # #

Concealed by heavy shadows on the porch, Chase and Dallas examined the windows for an alarm. They'd already cut the phone lines, but still needed to be careful not to trip a house alarm. Finding it, they realized it would be easy to bypass. Triggered by opening the window, they instead cut the flashing around the window panes and removed the center part of the window carefully. When they had enough removed, they crawled through instead of sliding the window open.

Chase figured this would be a simple job. Since they wanted the arson to be detected, they could be sloppy. Still, he knew the destruction had to be complete. Not only was the house to be destroyed, but Emma and Cathy also had to parish. To guarantee success, Chase brought six chemical bombs set to explode by a timer - his preferred method of arson. But unlike a typical explosive, these worked by chemical reactions. When the timer went off, chemicals would mix and create a powerful explosion spreading fire over a large area. After planting the devices around the downstairs and setting the timers, Dallas thought it would be a good idea to pull the gas line from the oven. This was not part of Chase's plan. Chase immediately smelled the gas and was pissed.

"What the fuck did you do?" he asked as loud as he dared.

"I thought it would help," Dallas whispered.

"You idiot! They might smell it. Come on, we need to take the old bitches out before they wake up," he said pointing to the stairs.

# # #

"Hey... hey lady. Are you ok?" a voice asked.

Feeling someone gently shaking her shoulder, Melony's eyes slowly fluttered open. When she was able to focus she saw a young couple looking down at her. Realizing she was on the ground she tried to get up, but was unsteady. She'd hit her head when she passed out and had a pounding headache.

"Are you ok?" the woman asked again.

"Did someone attack you?" the boyfriend asked. "Do you want me to call the police?"

"No, I wasn't attacked," she said. She held her head while trying to shake the dizzy feeling. The boyfriend opened his truck and asked if she wanted to sit on the seat.

"Oh my god!" she cried out remembering what she saw. This startled the couple. "What's wrong? Are you sure you're ok?" they asked again.

"I'm ok. Thank you. Thank you so much. I have to go," she said as she stood up and ran to the back entrance of the club.

When she entered, she found her sister, the club manager, and told her she needed to talk with Devan right away, it was an emergency. She was in luck, he was hosting a private party in the rotating lounge. Her sister brought Devan to her.

Melony insisted they talk in private so Devan led her to his office. Once there, she recounted her story.

"You're sure it was the same man from Pollock's office?" Devan asked.

"I'm certain. I noticed the scar on his face," she insisted.

Devan picked up his phone and tried to call Emma but only got a busy signal. He hung up then said, "I'm going to Emma's. You stay here, you'll be safe. If you don't hear from me in an hour, call the police and send them to the Carson House."

Melony's eyes were huge. She nodded in agreement. Then, the reality of what she'd witnessed hit her and she broke down. Devan put his arm around her to try and comfort her, but knew time was of the essence.

"One hour," he said pulling away from her. "If you don't hear from me in an hour call the police," he repeated and left his office.

Melony sat on the couch holding her head crying hysterically.

On his way to Emma's, he called Jamison and gave him a quick rundown.

"I don't like you going over there by yourself, Boss. Wait for me, I'm leaving now."

"I can't wait. She witnessed this over an hour ago. Who knows what's happened since? Just meet me there when you can."

"Be careful, Devan. We have no idea what that asshole is up to. If they really did kill Pollock, they won't think twice about taking you out either."

"I know, that's why I need you to get there as soon as possible. Why'd you have to buy a house so far out in the fuckin' country anyway?"

Chapter
35

Chase and Dallas quietly made their way up the stairs. When they reached the open landing, they split up to check each of the four bedrooms on this floor. Reuniting a few minutes later, they'd found Cathy and Emma. Dallas would take Cathy and Chase would take Emma.

# # #

Tor crossed the last deserted street and then ran down the sidewalk next to the wall surrounding Emma's block until he reached the opening. Squeezing through, he shot out into the yard and froze in place. Hearing Poe crying, he took off toward Thomas's cottage. When he got there, he found Thomas face down on the patio. A large pool of blood had accumulated next to his head. Poe was sitting in the doorway crying loudly. Tor's eyes ignited in a brilliant yellow green glow. He walked over to Thomas and nuzzled his neck. A visible glow radiated from Tor's eyes and was absorbed into Thomas. It was as if Thomas was breathing in the vaporous glow of Tor's energy. With each breath Thomas took, his raspy breathing began to improve. Then Tor heard the sound of something shatter and abruptly cut off the stream of energy. Thomas's breathing was better but he was still unconscious. Tor walked over to Poe and nuzzled him affectionately then turned and ran up the path. He stopped to look back at Poe, lightly meowing, he took off again running toward the house. Poe watched as Tor disappeared into the darkness.

# # #

Dallas quietly entered Cathy's room. The plan was to smother the women to death. Even though they hoped the fire would burn the bodies severely, they knew a stabbing or gunshot could be detected in an autopsy. Quietly taking a pillow from a nearby chair, Dallas approached. Looking at Cathy as she slept, he grinned a horrific grin then leapt upon her, forcing the pillow down hard on her face. Struggling violently, Cathy fought back kicking and scratching. In the struggle, she knocked a lamp to the floor, shattering it to pieces. She outweighed Dallas by an easy hundred pounds, but he had the advantage. All he had to do was hold on until she stopped moving. After about a minute, Cathy went limp. Dallas pulled the pillow away and could see in the pale light of the room her open lifeless eyes. Cathy had scratched his arms in the struggle. "Bitch! Look what you did to me!" he said seeing his arms. He spit on her before leaving the room.

Chase quietly entered Emma's room. Even though he knew the plan was to smother her in her sleep, his psychotic nature couldn't resist the opportunity to torment her first. The room was more illuminated than Cathy's because of a night light coming from a partially opened bathroom door. Suddenly a loud crashing sound came from Cathy's room. Emma immediately woke up to see Chase standing over her. Chase leapt on top of her and put his powerful hands around her neck. Holding her in place he couldn't resist gloating. "Mrs. Emma Perkins, the mayor says hello. Since you're soon no longer going to be in this world, I feel it's safe to tell you that he and I have fixed it so Pollock is going to be framed for your murder and the burning down of your beloved Carson House."

Letting what he said sink in, Chase released the pressure some on her neck. He wanted her conscious so he could see and hear her beg him for her life, but Emma had no intention of begging.

"You and that cowardly prick can go to hell!" she said through clenched teeth.

For a second Chase was startled by her response, but not for long. He struck her repeatedly across her face then gripped her neck with a vice like hold. "You think you're a tough old bitch? Well, you are putting up more of a fight than Pollock did. Sadly, he's no longer with us. Well, that's not completely true. His body is in the trunk of my car, but he'll never be found. Oh, and then we're going to set up your friend Mr. Ross so he takes the fall for this whole thing," Chase said smugly. "Time to die Mrs. Perkins. Tell Pollock hello for me when you see him." Chase tightened his grip for the kill. Emma struggled, but it was no use, darkness began closing in.

Tor shot through the open window and landed on the bed with his eyes glowing.

"What the fuck?" Chase pulled back from Emma.

Suffocating and drifting into unconsciousness from her crushed airway, Emma saw Tor leap on Chase, his eyes glowing brightly then she passed out.

Before Chase had a chance to react, Tor sank his claws and teeth into his face and neck. At the same time he threw off all restraints and drew in Chase's life force with ease. For Chase, it was like being struck by lightning. He was paralyzed, as helpless as an insect being drained dry by a spider. In a matter of seconds it was over. His lifeless body fell to the floor, eyes open. His face frozen in a mask of agony.

Tor jumped back on the bed with Emma. He approached her as he did with Thomas, eyes glowing fiercely and slowly exhaling energy into Emma. Badly injured and gasping for breath, she slowly began to breathe better as she inhaled the energy Tor was giving her.

All of a sudden the house was rocked by numerous explosions. Dallas appeared in the doorway.

"Chase! We gotta get out of here--" stopping in mid-sentence. He saw Chase's lifeless body on the floor. Before he could approach him, he was struck hard from behind by a baseball bat knocking him against the wall. Shaking it off, he turned to find Cathy standing there in mid swing. But this time he was able to catch the bat and slammed Cathy into the wall hard causing her to get knocked out and fall to the floor.

Dallas took the bat. Looking at Cathy he said, "Let's see you wake up from this." As he positioned himself over her to crush her head in, Tor leapt on to Dallas, sinking his teeth and claws into his back. As with Chase, Tor held on tight, draining Dallas's life force. Helpless and frozen in excruciating pain, Dallas felt his life rapidly draining from his body. In a matter of seconds it was over. He collapsed to the floor, eyes open, staring out into nothingness.

Tor approached Cathy gently pawing at her face trying to wake her but got no response, she was unconscious. Hearing Emma coughing, he returned to her bed, unaware a deadly fire was spreading downstairs.

Chapter
36

Seeing flames erupting form one corner of the house as he approached in his car, Devan knew time was running out. He raced down the street and straight toward the large steal double gates at the end of the road. Bracing for impact, he punched the accelerator and sent his car crashing into and through the gates. The impact was violent and completely destroyed the front end of his brand new Jaguar XF causing the airbags to deploy. Fortunately, the momentum was enough for the car to clear the gates and come to a rest in the yard not obstructing the driveway. A little dazed from the impact and airbag, Devan quickly shook it off and leapt from the car and ran toward the front door. The fire was raging, but so far was mostly contained to the back side of the house. Catching the sight of someone staggering out of the shadows he immediately recognized Thomas.

"Thomas!" Devan called out. He ran over to him. Thomas was covered in blood from a serious laceration on the back of his head, but he seemed to pay it no mind.

"Miss Cathy and Mrs. Emma are still in there!"

Nodding, Devan patted his shoulder. "Let's do this." They ran to the front porch and Devan kicked the doors open with one powerful kick. Heat and smoke burst out. Shielding their faces with their arms, Devan yelled over the roar of the fire, "Where would they be?"

"Probably upstairs. This way," Thomas said pointing toward the large curving staircase wrapping around the foyer walls.

They cleared three or four steps at a time. The foyer was brightly lit by the yellow glow of flames burning across the ceiling but the fire had not reached the stairs or walls yet. The smoke, too, seemed to be light, but Devan knew it was only a matter of time. The whole house was a tinderbox.

When they reached Emma's bedroom the sight was surreal. The room was an oven, brightly lit by the intense yellow glow of fire racing across the ceiling above them. The smoke, for the time being, was finding another way out giving a clear view of the devastation. Cathy was lying in the doorway. Emma was on the bed with Tor standing defiantly beside her, protecting her. Devan saw the bodies of two men and recognized the one from Pollock's office. In a split second he processed the scene. "Fucking Douglas!" He was in a fit of rage. Seeing the man's wallet and cellphone in his back pocket, he quickly grabbed them. Hearing the house crack and pop as the fire ravaged the structure, Devan refocused. Cathy moaned when he rolled her over. "She's alive! Thomas, can you carry her out?"

Not even answering he reached down and scooped her up in one sweeping motion. It was so quick, Devan was impressed. "Good man. Get her out of here. I'll get Emma," he shouted over the roar of the fire.

Though badly injured and himself unsteady, Thomas cradled Cathy in his arms and rushed her down the stairs and out of the house as good as any trained fire fighter would have done before collapsing unconscious a safe distance away in the grass.

Before Devan could make his way to Emma there was a loud cracking sound and then the house shook. Part of another bedroom had fallen through the ceiling and into the dining room below. Devan knew time was running out. The entire house was going to be consumed in a matter of minutes.

When he reached Emma, Tor's eyes ignited in defiance. Momentarily awestruck, Devan looked on in wonder. Are they really glowing or is that the reflection from the fire above? "It's ok, buddy, I'm here to help," Devan said gesturing to Tor with his hands. Tor's eyes returned to normal. But then the ceiling cracked violently. Devan managed to grab Emma and dove to the floor before a large flaming chunk of ceiling crashed down across the room and bed. When he stood up he realized the room had been cut in two by a massive flaming ceiling beam. A large dresser had also been knocked over blocking the open window. Tor was trapped on the other side. Noticing a bank of windows above Tor and the roof outside, he grabbed a small bedside table and threw it across the room and through the windows, shattering them and giving Tor a way to escape. "Go, Tor!!" Devan yelled over the growing flames and heat. "Get out!"

He scooped up Emma and ran to the stairs. Parts of the ceiling had dropped, but Devan was able to kick them out of the way as he raced down the stairs and out of the house before collapsing exhausted next to Thomas and Cathy in the yard. Looking back at the house now completely engulfed in flames, the fire reflecting in his eyes was nothing compared to the one burning within him. "Fucking Douglas," he said again under his breath.

Within seconds of reaching Thomas and Cathy, Devan heard the approaching fire trucks. They surrounded the block and immediately began trying to extinguish the fire. Still, it was too late for the old house. All they could do was contain it. Carson House was no more. Paramedics rushed over and immediately began administering first aid. Emma was still unconscious, but Cathy was recovering. Thomas had lost a lot of blood but was stable. Cathy was able to tell the paramedics his blood type. She even asked Devan to get Poe from Thomas' cottage and look after him for them.

In the rush to help save Emma and Cathy, Devan didn't notice he'd broken his wrist and had sustained several minor facial lacerations from the air bag. Refusing to go to the hospital, Devan retrieved Poe and waited for Jamison to arrive. Fortunately, Thomas had shut the door to his cottage before heading to the house leaving Poe safe inside. After being bandaged up by the paramedics he gave a statement to the police.

Devan gave a full accounting of the events from the time Melony came to him at the club. He even gave the police the wallet he lifted off the one man but kept the cellphone. He called Melony to let her know he was ok. He told her he'd be back soon and to stay there because the police wanted to take her statement.

"Holy shit, Devan! What happened? Is that your car?" Jamison asked through the lowered passenger window of his truck, pointing to the still smoldering Jaguar.

Devan loaded Poe into the backseat and climbed in. "Yeah, I kind of had to use it as a battering ram. I don't recommend it."

"Who's your little friend?"

"This is Poe. It appears I'll be looking after him for a while."

"So, what happened?" Jamison asked.

"I have no idea. Thomas and I raced in looking for the ladies. We found Cathy passed out in the hall upstairs. It looked like she might have fought with and possibly knocked out one of the attackers. The scar-faced guy from Pollock's office was lying on the floor in Emma's room. I couldn't tell how he died - maybe she shot him. Thomas and I barely had enough time to get them out before the whole thing went up in flames." He reached into his pocket he pulled out the phone he took off Chase. "Here. I lifted this off our scar-face friend. I need your intel buds to break into it ASAP. I want to know everything that fucker was up to," Devan said and handed Jamison the phone.

"I'm on it, Boss."

Looking out the window at the smoldering ruins of Carson House, Devan's eyes burned with rage. "That prick mayor was behind this and I don't think he acted alone. Given my recent injury," he said flexing his bandaged left wrist, "I'm going to need your help in persuading his honor and his pedophile father to talk. Are you up for it?"

Jamison's rugged facial features twisted into a sinister smile. "I got this."

Chapter
37

Jamison dropped Devan off at the club so he could be there for Melony if she needed him while giving her statement. It was a good thing he did. More than once she broke down trying to recall what she'd seen. After the police left, he thanked her again and had her sister take her home.

Linda met Devan at his office with a change of clothes so he could get cleaned up before they went to the hospital to check on Emma, Cathy, and Thomas.

Jamison was on his mission. After dropping Devan off and arranging for security to be stationed at Emma's, he took the phone to a buddy he knew would be able to access everything on it by morning.

# # #

Leaving little Poe at his office, it was well past midnight before Devan and Linda arrived at the hospital. Normally visitors would not be allowed at such a late hour but since Devan was one of the hospital's largest donors, they made an exception. Emma was still unconscious in ICU, but Thomas and Cathy had been moved to a private room.

They knocked on their hospital room door quietly. Cathy motioned for them to come in. They were surprised to find her wide awake. She had insisted on being in the same room as Thomas. Even though he was badly injured, he'd never been away from home. Knowing he didn't do well with strangers, she wanted to be there in case he got scared. When she saw Devan, she immediately perked up. Devan and Linda hugged her gently. Her head was wrapped in a bandage. Thomas was fast asleep in the other bed. He also had a thick bandage wrapped around his head. Given the severity of his injuries, Cathy wasn't taking any chances with the hospital staff. Referring to the late shift as "amateur hour" she was determined to stay awake and watch Thomas all night.

Curious and helping to pass the time, Devan asked her if she remembered what happened. To his surprise, she remembered everything in striking detail. She explained when she realized what was happening to her, she faked dying. It helped that she was a diver in the Navy and could hold her breath for a long time. Pretending to be dead, saved her life. After the guy left, she retrieved a baseball bat and went after him. Devan asked if she knocked him out, but she said no. She remembered hitting him once, but when she tried a second time, he grabbed the bat and slammed her into the wall. She had no idea what happened after that or why he was lying on the floor when they arrived.

Changing the subject, Linda had a way of turning any situation into a good time. She had Cathy laughing to the point of tears several times as she quietly talked about other topics in an attempt to lighten the mood. Both Devan and Linda respected Cathy and admired how devoted she was to Thomas and Emma. They wanted to be there for her. Finally, the nurse in Cathy kicked in. Realizing Devan was also injured, she thanked him again for saving their lives then insisted he go home and get some rest. She assured him she'd call him as soon as they had any news on Emma or Thomas. Reluctantly, they agreed and said their goodbyes. On the drive home Devan filled Linda in on everything.

"You really think the mayor was behind all this?" she asked.

"It would appear so."

"He can't be allowed to get away with it!" Her grip on the steering wheel tightened as she drove.

Seeing her knuckles turn white, he reached over and squeezed her hand. "Don't worry baby. He won't."

Chapter
38

Emma regained consciousness a few hours after Devan and Linda left the hospital. She immediately asked about Cathy and Thomas and was relieved to find out they were ok. A police officer had been stationed outside her room. When she was fully awake, he called the detective investigating the case and he came to the hospital. When the detective told her it was Devan and Thomas who rescued them, she broke down in tears. "Oh Thomas..." she said wiping the tears from her eyes. His devotion and love for her touched her deeply.

Emma was able to give a brief statement before her doctors made them cut it short. The detective was surprised by how much she could recall and was especially interested in knowing how the two intruders died. Unfortunately, she told him she did not know. The last thing she remembered was the man telling her it was time to die then he choked her unconscious. But before that, she told the detective the man bragged about killing Councilman Pollock and said they had his body in his car. She also told him they planned to set Pollock up to make it look like he and Devan had conspired to kill her and burn her house down. When he asked her if she could think of any reason why this man would do this, she said she had no idea. She'd never seen him before.

But Emma did know. She knew exactly who was behind it and why. Knowing the mayor and his family had considerable pull, she decided to keep this bit of information to herself for now. At the moment, it was her word against the mayor's . No, she knew this was not a matter for the police or legal system. She wanted justice. Real justice. And she knew Devan was the only one who could get it for her.

# # #

When Devan arrived at his office the next morning, he was surprised to find Jamison waiting for him.

"Jackpot!" Jamison said holding the phone Devan lifted off Chase.

"That good?"

"Oh yeah. It appears the mayor's flunky didn't think much of him either. He recorded all the conversations they had together. And I think you're going to love this one," Jamison said, pushing the play button.

Jamison played the conversation where Chase and the mayor meticulously planned Emma's and Pollock's murder, the arson, and how they planned to frame Pollock and Devan.

"I think it's time you and I have a conversation with John Jr. and Big Daddy," Devan said. "But, first, I'm going to the hospital to see Emma. Cathy called and said she was awake and wanted to see me as soon as possible.

Jamison nodded at his bandaged wrist, "How's that today?"

"Getting better and better by the minute."

# # #

Emma had been moved to a private room and was resting alone when Devan arrived.

"Devan! Thank you for coming," she said with a raspy voice. "From what I hear you and Thomas saved our lives. I can't thank you enough.

Humbled, he bent down to gently hug her. "No thanks necessary. I'm just happy to see that everyone is ok. By the way, should you be talking?" he asked pointing to her throat. He also saw the heavy bruising on her neck and face.

"Probably not but this can't wait," she said. She sat up to get more comfortable and motioned for him to come closer. She quietly told him what the scar-faced man said as he tormented her. Devan also shared what they got from the phone. He told her he'd already set up a meeting with the mayor and his father for 11:00a.m. at his office.

Emma's smiled. "Wish I could be there to see their faces when you tell them what you know. You have to promise to tell me everything. Don't leave out any details," she insisted.

Devan promised then remembered something. "I wanted to ask you. What happened to the guy who attacked you? When we got to you, he was lying on the floor dead. Did you shoot him?"

Emma frowned and shook her head. "I wish. But honestly, I have no idea. The detective who took my statement told me what you told him. I just can't remember." She paused for a second as if she was trying to recall something. "I do remember something strange, but I can't be sure it happened. It seems more like a dream."

Noticing she was having trouble talking, he offered her a cup of water which she happily took. After taking a sip she continued. "Call me crazy, but I swear I think Tor attacked the man. The last thing I think I remember seeing was Tor leaping on him. But..." She paused and thought for a moment. "But, no, it couldn't have been real."

"Why do you say that?" he asked seeing her confusion.

"Because what I saw couldn't have been real." She paused for a second, again collecting her thoughts. "I could have sworn when he attacked the man his eyes were glowing a bright yellow-green," she said staring at him dumbfounded.

Devan slowly nodded his head in agreement and smiled. "It was his eyes. I knew it!" he said. "You're not any crazier than I am. When I first tried to lift you off the bed, Tor bowed up protecting you and his eyes ignited in a bright yellow-green glow. I tried to convince myself it had to be the fire reflecting in them, but maybe not. They sure looked like they were glowing to me. He even appeared to turn it off when I told him I was there to help."

"Do you think Tor killed those men?" she asked

Devan shrugged. "If he did, that's one bad ass cat."

Emma smiled. "I knew he was special from the second he came to live with us. I just hope he's ok."

"When a large part of the ceiling fell he was trapped on the other side of your room. I threw a table through some windows so he could get out but I didn't see if he did."

Thinking to herself for a second Emma asked, "Can you please go by the house and see if you can find him. I have to know if he's ok. And little Poe, too. Thomas will be devastated if he lost both of them."

"I will. I promise. And don't worry about Poe, he's hanging out with me and Linda. Cathy told me about him before they loaded you guys into the ambulance."

"Oh, thank heavens," she said relieved.

"And speaking of Thomas, how's he doing?" Devan asked.

"Much better. Cathy is with him. He apparently likes the orange sherbet ice cream they have here a lot."

"That's great news, I'll swing by on my way out and say hello."

Devan and Emma discussed a few more details regarding his upcoming meeting with the mayor and his father before they said their goodbyes. As promised, he dropped in on Thomas and Cathy prior to leaving the hospital.

On his drive back to his office, Devan kept replaying his encounter with Tor over in his head. Did his eyes really glow? Could he have killed those men? "If that's truly the case, then he really is one bad ass cat," Devan said out loud as he drove on lost in thought.

# # #

Tor did survive the fire. After escaping through the broken window, he climbed down the tree and was making his way to the four of them on the lawn when the fire engines began to arrive with their sirens blaring. Startled, Tor took refuge in the shadows and bushes. From his vantage point, he watched as the paramedics treated everyone and loaded Emma, Cathy and Thomas into two waiting ambulances. After seeing Devan talking with

Cathy, Tor followed him to Thomas's cottage and watched him collect Poe in an animal carrier. Still unseen, Tor followed Devan, keeping to the shadows. He watched as a large truck pulled up outside the smashed front gates. He saw Devan load Poe into the back seat then he got in and the truck drove away. Tor sat in the shadows watching the firemen spray water on the burning house from all sides. There were also hoses on ladders from high above spraying torrents of water onto the fire. Even though their response was fast, the devastation was enormous. The house was a complete loss. For hours, Tor watched until the activity surrounding the smoldering ruins died off. Under the cover of darkness, Tor slipped out the front gates and on to the neighborhood streets. But, instead of heading to his familiar warehouse hunting grounds, he ventured into the city.

Reaching Main Street, Tor turned south and cautiously traveled toward the Main Street Bridge spanning the St. Johns River. Fortunately, it was early morning and the downtown streets were mostly deserted. Cautiously, Tor crossed a large intersection and ran up the pedestrian sidewalk onto the bridge. Spanning several hundred feet over the river, Tor quickly and carefully made his way across the bridge exiting into San Marco located on the city's Southside. After traveling a few blocks, he disappeared into a small residential area. Driven by instinct, Tor was on a mission only he could understand.

Chapter
39

As requested, JD arrived at Devan's office at exactly 11:00a.m. His son, the mayor, defiant as usual, was ten minutes late. Devan made the men wait for an additional ten minutes in the presence of Jamison and two other equally hard looking security personnel.

At 11:30, Jamison himself escorted them to Devan's office. Sitting at his desk when they entered, Devan saw a small red light discretely hidden on the backside of his desk turn on. Unseen by the others, Devan's eyebrow slightly raised. Reaching under his desk, he pushed another button. After a brief delay, the light turned green. Satisfied, he smiled at his guests and gestured toward two chairs for them to be seated. Jamison shut the office doors but did not leave the room. He took a seat on a couch against the wall behind the men.

Looking from one to the other, Devan said, "I'm not one for bullshit so I'll get right to the point. Did either of you have anything to do with Councilman Pollock's murder or the burning of Carson House and the attempted murder of Emma Perkins, her nurse and handyman?" Cutting them off before either could respond, he added, "And choose your next words very carefully."

"Of course not! Why would you think that? We have a deal, a good deal! Absolutely not!" JD tried to sound insulted, but the fear in his voice diminished the effect of his forced hardline response.

Devan shifted his gazed and looked directly at the John Jr. "And you?" he asked.

Red-faced, John Jr.'s frustration was obvious. He stayed quiet and looked toward the floor.

JD turned toward his son, eyebrows raised and mouth hanging open confused.

"Your silence is deafening, Your Honor. Are you sure you don't have anything you want to add to this conversation?" Devan asked. He sat back in his chair and stared at John Jr. with ice cold eyes. After what seemed like an eternity of silence, Devan spoke. "Let me tell you what I know gentlemen. When I got to Mrs. Perkins, I noticed one of the assailants lying on the floor. I took his wallet and cell phone. The police don't know about the phone." His eyes never left John Jr. "Fortunately for us, my associate behind you was able to retrieve some interesting information off that phone. It would appear this man didn't trust his accomplice very much and recorded all of their conversations. Understandable I guess. I mean when one is too much of a pussy to do his own dirty work, I guess it makes sense to take precautions." Letting what he said sink in, Devan enjoyed watching the color drain from John Jr's face.

Biting his lip, he refused to look Devan in the eye.

"One recording in particular was especially interesting to me. Jamison, would you do the honors please?" He motioned for Jamison to approach. Jamison produced the phone and stood between them. His 6'4" stature was intimidating enough, but standing so close made both men uneasy.

Jamison played the same recording he played for Devan earlier that morning. Ending it at an appropriate point, he returned to the couch and sat down.

JD sat speechless, mouth still hanging open, his disappointment overwhelmed him until he finally erupted. "Jr.! You fool! What the hell were you thinking? You goddamned fool! You've ruined us! We're finished! You selfish little shit! You've never cared about anyone but yourself. What the hell was going through that stupid head of yours?"

"Shut up JD!" Devan said slamming his good fist down on the desk. Looking at the mayor, Devan asked, "Do you have anything you want to add to this conversation?"

John Jr. sat slumped in his chair arms tightly crossed across his stomach still refusing to look at Devan or say anything. He remained defiantly silent.

"Let me tell you what's going to happen. Carson House is going to be rebuilt for Mrs. Perkins in record time. And JD, I expect your full cooperation in this matter. I don't give a shit what it costs or takes, if something is needed for that house it better be there no later than the next morning. Do I make myself clear? This is priority number one for all of us until it's finished. I will not tolerate any excuse."

"Of course, Devan. Anything," JD responded. He was cautiously optimistic that he and his family might still have a future in Jacksonville all while knowing Devan wasn't finished yet.

"And you, Jr.," Devan paused for an uncomfortable amount of time. "You disgust me. To be honest, I could give a shit about Pollock. He was your flunky. But using your hired thug to murder Emma and her family is beneath contempt. You're done in this town. You'll resign tomorrow. You have one week to take care of any business you have here then get the fuck out of this city. If you ever set foot in this town again for any reason, it'll be the last time you do." Pausing, Devan read his demeanor. He wasn't fearful, regretful, or even remorseful. He was mad. Mad because Chase screwed up and he got caught. Knowing he and Jamison might still need to deal with John Jr. in other ways at a later point, Devan subtly smiled at the thought of beating the shit out of him. "Now get the fuck out of my office."

John Jr. shot up from his chair and headed straight for the door. JD attempted to say something, but Devan cut him off. "Get out," he said. Nodding, JD quickly caught up with his son. Two guards escorted the men out of the building.

# # #

From the second they left Devan's office, JD ripped into him. Once outside, the mayor pulled his phone from his pocket. "Shut the hell up, Father!"

JD was speechless.

"I got the bastard! I finally got the bastard. I did something you've been too weak and scared to do for far too long! I recorded that entire conversation on my phone," the mayor said defiantly lashing out at his father.

"And just what do you expect to prove with that?"

"What do I expect to prove? I have him threatening me and strong-arming you into rebuilding the old bitch's house. We have him! He wouldn't want this out there anymore than we do. So fuck him! Fuck Devan Ross! I'm not resigning as mayor. No way!"

"Jr., you're an idiot. If you recorded everything then you also have the recording between you and that dumbass of yours. You'll still implicate yourself."

"I don't care! If I'm going down, then he is too. Fuck him!"

Confident, John Jr. pushed "Play" on the phone, but heard nothing. Only static. Slowly his cocky expression faded as he frantically searched for the recording. "That's impossible! I know it's here! It has to be here, I started it recording before I walked into the building..."

Irritated, JD waved him off. "Enough of this nonsense." He headed toward his car leaving John Jr. standing there desperately looking for the recording.

# # #

"That was strange, the asshole didn't say a word. What's up with that?" Jamison asked after JD and John Jr. left Devan's office.

"He was trying to record our conversation," Devan said. He poured himself a cup of coffee.

Jamison laughed. "See? I told you that jamming device would pay off."

Chapter
40

After JD and the mayor left, Devan went to the window and looked out. From his corner office he could see the back entrance of the club as well as a four-way intersection and, of course, the city skyline in the distance. Standing at the window sipping his coffee, he saw JD and John Jr. emerge onto the sidewalk. They seemed to be engaged in a heated discussion. He watched as John Jr. pulled out his phone and pointed to it repeatedly. Then they looked as if they were trying to listen to something. After a few seconds, JD waved him off irritated. He walked to his waiting car, got in, and was driven off. They mayor looked confused. He slowly walked down the sidewalk in the direction of the intersection frantically fumbling with his phone. Noticing an open manhole surrounded by orange caution cones in the center of the intersection, Devan's eye was drawn to a cat sitting calmly on the opposite corner across the street. He was surprised by how still it was sitting despite the continuous flow of traffic. The more he studied it, the more familiar it looked. It reminded him of Emma's cat. But that would be impossible, he thought to himself. There's no way it could be him; her house was on the other side of the river in Springfield.

Devan was about to turn away from the window when he saw the cat stand up and dart out into the road, crossing through the intersection diagonally to another corner. When it ran into the street, a car heading north on the right side of the road swerved left to avoid hitting the animal, cutting in front of an oncoming city bus. Reacting instantly, the bus driver swerved to his left in an attempt to miss the car. But when he did, the front right tire of the bus fell into the open man hole, violently jarring the bus and knocking the bus driver off his seat. Completely out of control, the bus headed straight for John Jr. as he continued to fumble with his phone.

Hearing the bus approach, John Jr. looked up, but it was too late. In a desperate attempt to stop the bus, he put his hands out to no avail. The entire weight of the bus smashed into him, crushing him into the building, killing him instantly. Momentarily stunned by what just took place before him, Devan noticed the cat calmly sitting on the opposite corner looking on at the carnage. Recovering quickly, Devan nodded toward the cat and raised his cup, "Well done, Cat. Well done."

"What the hell was that?" Jamison asked springing to his feet after hearing the horrific crash and feeling the building shake.

Devan turned to him with a cocky smile. "Karma, my friend. That was Karma." He calmly took a sip of coffee before turning back to look out the window. Noticing that the cat was gone, he raised his coffee cup in the direction it had been sitting and again said, "Well done, Cat."

Chapter
41

Two days after leaving San Marco, Tor arrived at his destination. He'd made his way to a small residential neighborhood about two miles south of San Marco. Casually walking down a quiet street, he heard voices and people splashing in a pool at one particular house. Recognizing one of the voices, Tor ran up the drive way and then disappeared into a jungle of wildly over grown vegetation straddling a chain-link fence separating this house from another. The house was laid out in such a way that it bordered a small deep creek leading to the St. Johns River. The overgrowth had been left on purpose for privacy. Despite the neighborhood's close proximity to downtown, the large old trees and dense vegetation gave the impression of being in a secluded wilderness sanctuary. Determined to get to the other side of the fence, Tor jumped to the top but in the process snagged his collar on a sharp metal spike. Designed to break-away in just such a situation, Tor fought back using his eighteen-pound body as leverage. Pulling back, he snapped the collar freeing himself. Pivoting atop the fence, Tor listened to the voices. Hearing the one that sounded familiar again, he jumped to the ground. Broken, the collar fell off into the leaves. From inside the dense canape of underbrush, Tor watched as people swam and hung out on the pool deck. Cautiously observing his new surroundings from the safety of the dense underbrush, Tor was content. Little did he know, but another adventure was about to begin...

For more Tor, check out "Tor & The Immortals"

For more Devan Ross, check out "The American Way"

Printed in Great Britain
by Amazon